REDEMPTION

BOOKS BY HOWARD FAST

Howard

REDEMPTION

Fast

HARCOURT BRACE & COMPANY

New York   San Diego   London

Library of Congress Cataloging-in-Publication Data
Fast, Howard, 1914–
Redemption: a novel/Howard Fast.
p.   cm.
ISBN 0-15-100455-2
I. Title.
PS3511.A784R44   1999
813'.52—dc21   98-41373

Designed by Linda Lockowitz
Text set in Spectrum
Printed in the United States of America
First edition
F E D C B A

To Rachel, who has been down the track

REDEMPTION

CHAPTER ONE

Wall Street

May 25, 1996

IT HAD BEEN a quiet night in the detectives' squad room at the first precinct of the New York City Police. Sergeant Hull and Detective Flannery, homicide's midnight shift, sat at facing desks. Flannery was doing a crossword puzzle on the computer and Hull was typing a report on an ancient Underwood typewriter; and both men yawned, first one and then the other, as if the act were contagious. Hull was a tall, skinny man in his forties. He wore reading glasses down at the end of his long nose. Flannery was chubby, pug nose and red hair, and enthralled with their new computer, which Hull stubbornly refused to use. "You're a Luddite," he once said to Hull—to which Hull replied, "What in hell is a Luddite?" He didn't do crossword puzzles.

It was Saturday, May twenty-fifth, 1996, and if the midnight shift passed with no lethal violence, both men could look forward to the rest of the weekend off. Since it was now almost one A.M., their chances were good. The station was at 16 Ericsson, at the tip of Manhattan, pretty much closed down now and quiet as a graveyard.

Flannery frowned at his puzzle and said to Hull, "That new uniform downstairs, Annabelle—you know who I mean—you think she's got a guy?"

"How the hell should I know?"

"I thought you might have noticed," Flannery said. "How do you spell *restaurant*—*au* or *ua*?"

"*Au*. She's stacked. Good-looking. But with all this harassment stuff going around, how do you start?"

"Ask her for a date."

The telephone rang. Hull picked it up, listened for a moment, and then said, "OK, Lieutenant. We're on our way."

"What?"

"They got us one, and there goes the damn weekend. A banker or something, shot through the head, at Garson, Weeds and Anderson."

"Who phoned it in?"

"Your Annabelle. The boss told her to leave everything just as it is."

"Well, you win some and you lose some," Flannery said. "They're in the Omnibus Building, aren't they?"

"That's right."

When the detectives got to the Omnibus, the ambulance was already there. Two tired men with a stretcher stood next to Annabelle, who was twenty-four years old, blond, and six feet tall. A third man identified himself as Alec Prosky, a part of the weekend cleaning staff and the person who found the body.

"It's on the seventeenth floor," Annabelle informed them, a bit shaken and excited by her first homicide. "Prosky here's a cleaner, one of six in the building. His boss, Goober here, put in the 911." Goober grinned at them.

"Who's up there?"

"Kennedy, my partner," Annabelle said.

The two detectives, Annabelle, and Prosky entered one of the bank of elevators and rode up to the seventeenth floor. Hull asked where the other cleaners were, and Prosky answered that they were working other floors and probably didn't know of the crime. Garson, Weeds and Anderson occupied the whole of the seventeenth floor, and each man in the cleaning team did a floor by himself. He, Prosky, had touched nothing. Hull told Prosky to go down to the lobby and wait for the forensic team and then to bring them up.

"The building was locked?" he asked Prosky.

"Friday, it locks up at seven. We have the key and we come in at midnight."

"And the staff? The concierge and the others?"

"They leave by seven. Any late people let themselves out and close the front door behind them. We come in at midnight, and we set the alarm system when we leave."

"Real smart," Flannery observed. "So there's no alarm system while the cleaners are here."

Prosky shrugged, went into the elevator, and the doors closed. The three were in the reception room— eighteenth-century colonial wallpaper, leather upholstery, and walnut walls. A cherry-wood desk for the receptionist, and on the floor a large, pale blue Aubusson rug, matched by a specially woven runner that carpeted a long hallway. "He's at the end of it," Annabelle said, and led them down the hallway past several offices, a huge room of desks, telephones, and screens, then through this room to another corridor leading into more offices. Kennedy, Annabelle's partner, was waiting for them. He was a man in his late forties, weatherworn enough to do away with Flannery's fear of competition. The door to the office behind Kennedy was open.

"Cold as ice," Kennedy said. "He must have been put down hours ago."

"You didn't touch anything?" Hull demanded.

"Would I? I felt his cheeks."

The plate of the door said WILLIAM SEDGWICK HOPPER.

"He's been in the news," Annabelle said. "Something of a world figure. Two gold medals in the seventy-two Olympics. Lately, he's been involved in some kind of con. No charges and no arrest."

Hopper's office was businesslike: a desk, three telephones—each with multiple lines—a computer, and a comfortable desk chair facing the door, away from a fine view of the upper bay and the Statue of Liberty. Paneled walls, no pictures, three Signer-style chairs, and a couch. A door on the left led into a small bathroom with a liquor bar beneath the sink. The entire room was carpeted in rich mossy green.

Hopper was slumped forward on the desk, a fountain pen still clutched tightly over a checkbook in his right hand, and a trickle of blood down the back of his neck from a small hole at the base of his skull. He wore a shirt—collar open—a vest, and no tie. On the desk was a length of paper torn from the fax, about eighteen inches long. On the bottom of this sheet lay a twenty-two automatic Colt pistol, and printed on the paper, above the pistol, in red block letters: SWEET JOURNEY, BILLY.

Carefully Hull drew the checkbook from under the clenched hand. A check—still in the book, with no notation on the stub to identify it—was made out to cash, for the sum of one hundred thousand dollars. The check was unsigned.

"This is a doozy," Flannery said. "Whoever wasted him wanted the kill more than he wanted the money."

Standing at the doorway, Annabelle said, "Forgive me, Detective. Not 'he'—*she.*"

Looking at her, curious, Hull asked, "Why 'she'?"

"Because the cheerful good-bye note was written with lipstick."

"You're sure, Officer?"

"Pretty sure."

"Could you tell us the name of the lipstick?"

"Maybe. I could make a guess. Devlon's Autumn— very big last season."

"You got to be kidding," Flannery said.

"It's just a guess. I'm a blond, so I use that color. I've tried it, and it's just right. It goes better with a fair-haired woman—blue eyes, blond hair. You know, you try them all until you find one that fits your taste."

"Interesting," Hull admitted. "That would mean she stood behind him with the gun and watched him write the check. Then, before he could sign it, she decided to pop him. Either she's as rich as God or she hates his guts."

"A hundred thousand clams are a lot of hate," Flannery said.

"Cash. What the hell good is a check drawn to cash? He could stop it first thing Monday morning. Or maybe a man decided to use his wife's lipstick. This is one large, good-looking stud . . . blond hair—we got to find out a little about him, but that will wait for tomorrow. Forensics will match up the lipstick; and we'll find out about the women who work here."

"The blond hair's a rinse," Annabelle said.

Flannery regarded her with appreciation.

"So he was a happy hunter," Hull said. "Manhattan South will send their fingerprint team along with forensics, but my guess is she wore gloves. You agree, Officer?" to Annabelle.

"I would think so."

Flannery took a piece of tissue from the box on the desk, then picked up the gun and smelled it. "Still stinks. It's got its registration mark, so it's probably stolen and resold. We got to talk to Prosky. How many did he say were on the cleaning team?"

"Six," Annabelle said.

"I don't think there's anything there," Flannery said, touching the dead man's cheek. "They come in at midnight. My guess is that he's been dead at least five, six hours."

This was for the benefit of Annabelle. Hull did not contradict Flannery, and Flannery decided to ask Annabelle whether she had a steady boyfriend.

Her answer cheered him, and he decided to ask her about the two gold medals.

"I follow sports," Annabelle replied. "Javelin and shot put."

"Oh." Flannery was not quite certain what a javelin was. "Some kind of spear?"

"Some kind of spear," Annabelle agreed.

CHAPTER TWO

The Woman on the Bridge

March 16, 1996

Driving from New Jersey to New York, crossing the George Washington Bridge at half past three in the morning, I saw a woman standing at the rail of the pedestrian walkway, her back to me. I had spent the day with two old friends who taught at Rowan College—one a professor of social psychology and the other a physicist—and we had sat at the dinner table, immersed in good talk and ripe contention, until well after midnight. Rowan is in South Jersey, but after midnight the roads are empty and I had made good progress.

Ordinarily I would have been sound asleep at this hour; but I was full of ideas and odd thoughts, alert and awake, and when I noticed the woman, I braked and slid to a stop against the walkway. There was little traffic on the bridge. A woman alone at that ungodly hour was something I could not ignore. Stopped about a dozen feet from her, I said, "I wouldn't, if I were you. It might not kill you at all, and that would leave you with months of agony in the hospital—worse than whatever pain you're in now."

Of course it would have killed her, but that was all I could invent at the moment. She turned to face me. In the sallow gleam of the bridge lights, I couldn't see her too clearly, but I had the impression of a good-looking woman in her forties with shoulder-length, flaxen hair, gray eyes, and every inch of her filled with woe. That was just an impression. She wore a blue coat that fell below her knees. For perhaps a minute she remained silent, staring at me. She saw a man of seventy-eight years, gray haired with glasses, wearing a tweed jacket and gray flannels. I expected anything, rage, hostility, fear, bitterness—perhaps a rush to the railing to get it over with. But after that very long minute or so of silence, she asked softly, "How did you know?"

Not Who are you? or What business is it of yours? or Why don't you go away and leave me alone?—but simply that soft, almost gentle question.

"Because I've opened that door a hundred times."

"What door?"

"The door you are looking at."

"Who are you?"

The important thing was to keep her talking. I could already hear the scream of a Port Authority patrol car, and another part of my mind was planning how I would deal with that.

"A harmless old professor emeritus. A widower who has discussed suicide with himself many times. I reject it—in myself and in others. That's somewhat arrogant, but there it is."

At that moment, the patrol car pulled up behind mine, and the officer got out. He looked thoughtfully at the two of us, his hand on the butt of his gun, and then asked, "Broken down?"

"No. My daughter and I stopped to have a look at the river at night."

The woman was facing us and listening intently.

"Can I see your license?"

I took out my wallet, pulled out my license and my Columbia University ID, and handed the cards to him. He peered at them.

"You know it's illegal to park on the bridge, Professor."

"I realize that. I thought at this hour of the morning—"

"The trucks ride this lane, morning and night. I'll let you go with a warning. Now, please move your car."

I opened the passenger door of my car, wondering

what the woman would do and trying to recall whether attempted suicide was a crime in New York State. She hesitated, then slowly climbed over the divider, walked to the car, and got in. I entered the other side and started the motor, and still she said nothing.

"What's your name?" I asked her as we drove across the bridge.

"Hopper." Hardly more than a whisper, which set me to thinking of how much difference there is between death and life, in the mind. She had looked over the railing and felt the icy wind on her face as she plunged toward the water, and she was filled with the terrible passage between life and whatever lies beyond. I wondered what had been inside of her before she accepted death.

"I mean your first name," I said.

"Elizabeth. My name is Elizabeth Hopper."

"My name is Isaac Goldman," I told her. "Where do you live? Where should I take you?" The moment I asked the question, I regretted it. I felt it was irresponsible, that she should not be left alone as long as she was in the grip of a suicidal condition. The obvious answer was to take her to a hospital, but I didn't know her and didn't want to deliver the explanation a hospital would ask for—I knew nothing about her. I am not a physician; I am a professor of contract law. I had glanced at her enough by now to see her face. No one just plucked from a journey to death looks beautiful, but she had good features—a warm, full mouth, some lines and wrinkles—probably in her forties.

She answered the question by saying nothing, and I made the best decision I could under the circumstances. "Elizabeth, I'm going to take you home with me. I live on Riverside Drive between 115th Street and 116th Street. I've lived there for forty years. I'm an old widower. I have an extra bedroom. I feel that you need to be with someone. If you feel uneasy about my offer, I can take you wherever you wish, but I assure you that you will be safe with me."

"It doesn't matter," she said bleakly.

I drove home then, and Gregory, the night man, put my car away. He said nothing about the woman who was with me; lonely years had stamped me with respectability beyond comment. It was still dark, and the empty streets had that forlorn, abandoned look that New York takes on in the few hours before dawn when the night is over and the next day has not yet begun. Like most of the buildings on the Drive, ours had converted to self-service elevators. I lived on the seventh floor.

Still, Elizabeth Hopper had said not a word. But at my door she paused and for the first time really looked at me, a long, tired look. "Perhaps I ought to go home—"

"If you wish." I nodded. "I can call you a cab. But if

you're as tired as I am, you'll be more comfortable in the guest room. It used to be my son's room, before he went to college. He's married now. I have three grand-children—" I wasn't just chattering. I know something about depression, and I had already decided that before I let her go off, I'd call 911, not a taxi. In a manner of speaking, a person in deep depression has already be-gun the separation from life. The will to live sinks, and at its lowest level, there is no door open but suicide.

"Come inside," I said, unlocking the door. I switched on the lights, and she followed me through the foyer into the living room. She looked around and murmured, "It's very nice."

"Will you stay?"

"You don't know anything about me."

"I know that you're very tired and you need sleep. Come with me," I said gently. She followed me into the guest room. "It has its own bathroom," I explained, opening that door. "The bed is made up."

She nodded.

"There's a robe behind the bathroom door."

"Thank you, Professor. I'll leave in the morning."

"If you wish, of course. Perhaps you'd like a glass of warm milk? It would help you sleep."

She shook her head. "I don't know who you are or why you are being good to me," she said softly, "but I'm so tired I could sleep in the gutter. Thank you, Pro-fessor."

She closed the door behind her. I had done what I could do, short of calling the police. Going into the living room, I dropped into an easy chair, realizing that I had taken her to my place so that she might not escape—but why not let her escape? The answer was simple: I couldn't allow her to leave her death on my hands. I heard her toilet flush, and I heard the creak of the bed as she fell into it. Then I washed my face and hands, found a glass of cold milk in the fridge, and drank it down. Back in the living room, I fell into the easy chair once again. Stuffing my pipe but not lighting it, I remembered that when my wife was alive, I smoked only in my own office. Still, I didn't light the pipe but simply sat and looked at it, reflecting on this sad little drama that I had stepped into.

I fell asleep in the chair, and the next thing I knew, a voice was asking, "Professor?"

Elizabeth stood in front of me, dressed and with her coat on. The sun was pouring through the windows behind me.

"I couldn't leave without saying thank you again."

Stiff and cramped, I got myself out of the chair. "Good heavens, what time is it?"

"Ten o'clock," she responded.

"How do you feel?" I asked her.

"All right. Better than last night. I'll go home now. I'll be all right."

"No." I rubbed my eyes. "Forgive me, I don't often

fall asleep like that. A bit stiff. But I think we should talk."

She shook her head. "There's nothing to talk about. I'm over it."

"Yes, I'm sure," I said, thinking that she was by no means over it. My impression of her the night—or the morning—before, was of a woman wrapped in distress and agony. She looked different now. I could see the white in her hair; her gray eyes were alert, and the translucent skin that people of her coloring have now looked less ghostly. About five feet six inches in height, she was not beautiful as we think of beauty. But she had strong, even features. She might have come into my life late the night before and now just walk out of it, through the apartment door. Then I might never have seen her again, except to read in the morning paper that her body had been found. I am not a religious man, but I recall that it is said somewhere—in the Talmud, I believe—that he who saves a life saves the whole world. I think it is also said that when a life is saved, the obligation is put not upon the one who is saved but upon the one who acts to save.

I didn't ask her to stay. She was all negative at this point. I simply said, "You are free to leave, of course, but I want you to have some coffee first, and some breakfast. That is a small favor that I can claim for having saved your life."

"For what it's worth, Professor."

"And, for heaven's sake, don't call me 'Professor.' Call me Ike."

For the first time since I met her, she smiled. Her face changed; for a moment it glowed and then the glow was gone and she was looking at me searchingly.

"All right," she said. "I'm not being very pleasant. You're absolutely right. You saved my life. I would have done it, but I won't do it again. Do you live here alone—in this big place?"

"All alone. We bought the apartment some forty years ago, when I got my first teaching job at Columbia. It was very inexpensive then. Well, what wasn't? When my wife died three years ago, I simply went on living here. My memories are here. At my age, you don't have much more than that—looking backward."

She was staring out of the living-room windows, where the view opened onto the Hudson River. One of the old Dayline ships was chugging by, and closer to the Jersey shore, a tanker, high in the water, was putting out toward the harbor and the sea. The wind made the river choppy, and each small wave was topped with a golden glint of sunlight.

"It's so beautiful," she said.

"Yes—it is. The first time I considered doing what you were thinking of last night, I looked out of those windows, as I had a thousand times before."

She nodded.

"Breakfast, Elizabeth. Not philosophy. We don't

know each other well enough for that. I make coffee, and I have milk and dry cereal, four different kinds. The coffee's instant and I cheat by making it in the microwave."

She had two cups of coffee and two bowls of cornflakes and sliced banana. One of the nicer things about my age is that women trust you; they figure that the libido has shrunk to a point beyond threat. She asked what I had taught, and I explained that I was a lawyer who avoided both clients and courtrooms by teaching contract law in a university law school. She was well educated, college and then a master's in American art. She wanted to talk. That didn't surprise me. People talk to me easily. She talked to me about the day that led up to the bridge. She talked about her failed marriage, but the last straw was quite literally a matter of Lalique goblets. Life is filled with non sequiturs.

Her divorced husband, a broker on Wall Street, had come to her apartment unannounced the day before. It began with a gold bracelet. Her mother, who had died six years ago, had left her some money—almost all of it gone by now. Elizabeth had married the son of wealthy parents; and the heavy bracelet, which had cost her three thousand dollars, was a gift to him on the first anniversary of their wedding. Three thousand dollars for a bracelet was outside my scale of values and probably outside of hers, as well; but in her husband's world the scale was different, and I didn't interrupt.

Her husband had a fancy for gold jewelry, but he never wore the bracelet she had given him. She took to wearing it herself. Now he remembered it, and he came for it.

"It was the last indignity," she said. "No, the goblets were the last—but you don't want to listen to this."

"I do."

"I'm keeping you from your work. I'm a stranger to you. I don't know why I'm here talking about these things." She rose to look around for her coat.

"I have no work," I said gently. "Please don't go—not yet—please. I have an obligation to you."

"What obligation? You kept me from a stupid suicide. I have an obligation to you; you have no obligation to me."

"Have you been able to talk to anyone else about this?"

"No."

"It's very important that you talk—important to you and to me, as well."

"Ike," she said, but she was having difficulty with the name. "You do want me to call you Ike?"

"Yes."

"Why don't you let me go?"

"Good heavens, I'm not keeping you here. Put it to my curiosity about goblets."

Her question answered itself; she didn't want to go.

The world was full of waifs who were no responsibility of mine, and she was a waif—no question about that—beaten and broken, unable to walk away from the only man who had shown a touch of kindness and interest. Did I want to keep her here with me? That's a question I have asked myself a thousand times. I was lonely—but that had been the sum and whole of every day of my life since my wife had died. Some trick of fate or fortune had brought us together; and for very different reasons—or perhaps for the same reason—neither of us was willing to break the fragile link between us.

"Sit down and tell me about the goblets," I said to her, pouring another cup of coffee.

She sat down at the table again, and I think we both knew at that moment that we were trapped. Perhaps that's the wrong word. I have to say that my heart went out to her. I said to myself, Ike, this is a sick woman, a battered woman, and if you don't stop this right now, your life is going to become very complicated.

"Did you give him the bracelet? And by the way, what's his name?"

"Sedge. William Sedgwick Hopper. No!" The last word came out explosively. "No, I did not." Then she appeared to be ashamed of the small outburst. "It wasn't that. He said he'd get it sooner or later. I don't care about the damn bracelet."

"You're not wearing it," I noted.

"No. It's crazy—I didn't want to destroy it. I left the bracelet at home."

"It's not so crazy."

"But I wanted to destroy myself."

"Perhaps, perhaps not. I don't know you well enough to know what you wanted. Tell me about the goblets."

"Goblets?"

"You said that was the last straw."

She managed to smile. When she smiled, her whole face lit up and she was quite lovely. "You really want to hear about it? It makes me out to be a fool. I broke down when he told me he was going to leave me and marry Grace. She was my friend, and they had been sleeping together for months. I knew and I didn't want to know. I felt so cheap and dirty, like one of those incredible people on the afternoon talk shows." She began to cry at that point. I let her cry, only pushing a box of tissue toward her.

It was well past noon now, and the telephone rang, a colleague of mine at the university. I picked up the phone in the living room, and Elizabeth went into the bedroom where she had slept. As I put down the telephone, she came out of the bedroom with her coat on and her bag in her hand.

"Thank you for everything," she said.

"I would like to see you again, at least to hear about the wine goblets," I said.

"Yes, that would be nice."

"What will you do now?"

"Just go home. I work a swing shift. . . . Sometimes it's in the afternoon, sometimes in the evening when the store's open late, and sometimes it's in the early morning. It just depends. Today it's the afternoon shift, so I'll just have time to shower and change my clothes. I'll be all right."

"I thought we might have lunch together," I said lamely.

"You're really afraid that I'll try to kill myself again. I died once on the bridge. No, not again, Ike."

"Then dinner tonight? Later, after work? I want to see you again."

A long hesitation—as she stood at the door, her eyes cast down. Then she looked at me, her gray eyes filled with need, and slowly nodded. I wrote down her phone number and address, and then she left.

I shaved, showered, changed my clothes, and then walked over to the university, wondering if I should have canceled my lunch date with Charlie Brown, a colleague and old friend, or whether I should have brought Elizabeth with me. Charlie, a dozen years younger than I, was still teaching. His field was psychology. We lunched together every few weeks or so.

Charlie was a large, fleshy man, who loved anything that could be fried; he had never suffered a heart attack. He had an M.D., but he was too uneasy with the sight of blood to practice medicine. He had a wife and various children and was as close to contentment as you find these days. In the faculty dining room, he ordered a corned beef sandwich, and I had a salad.

"Ike," he greeted me, "you look great—ten years younger. What's happened?"

"I slept in a chair from five in the morning until ten."

"Oh? Then it's good for you. A lot of old folks sleep in chairs. Is this something new?"

I told him the story of the night before, and he listened without interrupting me. When I had finished, he swallowed the last of his deplorable sandwich, stared at me for a long moment, and then said, "God be praised, Ike, you're in love."

"What!"

"You're taking her to dinner tonight. You opened your home to her. She could have walked off with the family jewels—if you have family jewels. Did you count the money in your wallet?"

"This was a suicidal woman," I exclaimed indignantly. "What was I to do—have her death on my conscience?"

"That's bullshit," Charlie said.

"No, telling me that I'm in love is bullshit."

The waiter took away Charlie's plate, and replaced it with a piece of apple pie. "You could have taken her to the hospital. You could have called me. No, no—still and all, you did the right thing. You let her sleep, and then you fed her and showed compassion. Compassion is the best medicine we have for depression."

"I feel guilty because I let her go."

"Don't. She's not going to try it again. I do know something about depression and suicide. How long is it since Lena died?"

"Only three years."

"Only three years. Have you looked at another woman since then? You could still be working—but no, you live like a hermit."

"I'm seventy-eight, and I am not in love with Elizabeth Hopper. I know nothing about her. I crossed paths with her and it left me with an obligation."

"What did you say her name is? Elizabeth Hopper? Recently divorced?"

"Yes. Does that ring a bell with you?"

"Do you read the financial section of the *New York Times*?"

"No. Why should I? What I have is in U.S. bonds and some IBM stock I bought a lifetime ago; and I have a decent pension."

"Did she mention her husband's first name?"

"Yes—she did. William."

"It's a small world, Ike. There's a William Sedgwick

Hopper, one of the partners in the Wall Street firm of Garson, Weeds and Anderson. Neck deep in some kind of a scandal—millions of dollars. He was involved in one of those neat, complicated trading schemes. I don't know the ins and outs of the deal, but if you're interested, I can put you together with Harvey Goldberg in Business Administration. If you're going on with this affair, you should certainly know where the water's deep and where it's shallow."

"There is no affair in the picture, and I have no great interest in William Sedgwick Hopper. I'd be better served, Charlie, if you kept this to yourself. In confidence."

"Oh, absolutely," Charlie said.

That evening, I set out to pick up Elizabeth Hopper for dinner. I had called her half an hour before, and she sounded, if not cheerful, at least more alert and alive than she had in the morning. She lived in one of those high-rises on West Ninety-sixth Street, a one-room studio with a tiny kitchen—more of a closet than a kitchen—for which she paid fourteen hundred dollars a month. It was spartanly furnished: a studio pullout bed, serving by day as a couch; a sort of Chinese rug; a wooden table and four chairs; and a bamboo easy chair. On the wall, there was only a large framed photo of an older woman, possibly her mother.

Elizabeth wore a simple black dress; the smile with which she greeted me made her quite pretty. As I looked around the place, she said, "No, don't—please. It's dreadful. I hate it. I hate high-rises, and I don't have a view of anything except other people's windows. Will you sit down and have a glass of wine?"

"Sure," I agreed.

She had set out on the table a bowl of nuts and some crackers and cheese. She poured two glasses of white wine, and then she handed me an envelope, unsealed. "It's for you, Professor Ike. I lost my nerve, and I couldn't face thanking you anymore—"

"No, no, no," I said. "I can't have dinner with someone who calls me Professor Ike. Just Ike. That may be hard for you, but you'll get used to it."

"All right, Ike. In the letter I call you Ike. I'm much better, Ike. After I wrote the letter, I went out and bought the nuts and other stuff; and when I came back here, I was going to tear up the letter. But then I realized that I could never say to you, face-to-face, the same thing, and I think it ought to be said. So will you read it?"

"Of course," I agreed. I rose and went to the easy chair, where the light was better, and took the letter out of the envelope. Her handwriting was small but cursive and clear.

Dear Ike,

I was unable to thank you properly, because I am not good with words, especially when it comes to gratitude. You saved

my life, for whatever it is worth. How do you thank someone
for saving your life? What have they saved? I grew up in
Boston. I majored in art at St. Mary's College. I know a little
about depression. When I woke up in the morning in your son's
bedroom and looked out of the window at the Hudson River, I
suddenly understood something I had never understood before. I
saw what God had given me as a reward for being alive. I
don't know if that makes any sense to you, but I was raised in
a convent school, and suddenly I understood what the Sisters
meant when they drove home the fact that suicide was a sin
against God. I don't think I'm clinically depressed, but this is
for you, not me. I think you are the kindest man I ever met and
may God bless you for it. If I should do something terribly
foolish, please forgive me. But now that I have written this, I
don't think I will.

> *With gratitude and affection,*
> *Elizabeth Hopper*

I don't cry easily, even at dog films, but I was close
to it now. "May I keep this?" I asked her.

"If you wish."

I thanked her and folded the letter into my pocket.
"I made a reservation for seven-thirty at Romer's. Have
you eaten there?"

"Yes. I like it."

"It's quiet. We can talk."

She was hungry, and she ate well. She had not

eaten since breakfast at my apartment. She said something about paying for the dinner herself, but when I insisted that she was my guest, she put the effort aside. As I discovered, she did not have enough money in her purse to pay for the dinner, and her ex-husband had managed to cancel her charge cards. She had lamb chops, baked potato, and green beans, and she ate everything. I was pleased with that; suicidal intentions do not thrive on a full stomach. I watched her as she ate. With the grief quieted, she was a good-looking woman with regular features and large, deep gray eyes. Her figure was tight and strong. I must confess that I felt attracted to her, and it had been a long time since I felt attracted to any woman.

Over our coffee, I said to her, "Tell me about the wine goblets."

She shrugged. "You'll laugh at me."

"I'll never laugh at you," I promised.

"He's a very rich man, a millionaire many times over. The agreement was that he would pay me two thousand dollars a month—but that's complicated. I was in utter misery when he made the agreement, and I simply signed anything his lawyers brought to me. I would have signed my own death warrant to get away from him. That was in Manhattan, where he bought an expensive apartment after we left Boston."

I wanted to ask her a number of questions: How

could a millionaire divorce her with a payment of twenty-four thousand a year? Did she have a lawyer of her own? But I didn't want to interrupt her.

"When I refused to give up the gold bracelet, he brought up the question of the wine glasses. It was a very expensive set, a wedding present. When we separated, I took nothing except a few dishes. Don't ask me to explain that tonight, Ike, not tonight. I can't explain why he hated me and how much he hated me. Tonight is my first hour of happiness in a long time, and I treasure it. But I will tell you about the goblets. They were a wedding gift from my mother. My father had gone long before. She spent a great deal more than she could afford. When I moved to my apartment in New York I counted twelve crystal goblets, which I thought was half, and took them. He was not at home then, and I didn't count the whole set, and didn't know that one goblet had been broken. And after that awful quarrel the other night about the bracelet, he accused me of stealing twelve of the set and leaving only eleven for him. I was half hysterical by then—it doesn't seem possible, but it was only yesterday—and I went into the kitchen and took a goblet of the set and handed it to him. Do you know what he said?"

"Tell me."

"He said, 'Slut, I'm going to teach you a lesson in equity.' Slut was his favorite name for me. Then he took the Lalique wine glass and broke it against the kitchen sink. He put half the pieces in his pocket and left the rest in the sink, and told me he would get the bracelet, too. Then he left. Does it make any sense, Ike, that I should want to take my life over a wine goblet?"

There were tears in her eyes now. "Does it make any sense, Ike?" she pleaded.

I nodded.

"How does it make sense?" she whispered.

"It makes sense because you didn't take your life."

"Because you saved me."

"Perhaps—perhaps not. Very little in this life we live today makes sense."

I called the waiter and paid the check. We left the restaurant and walked north on Broadway. At this time, a quarter to eleven in the evening, upper Broadway was alive with the kind of human presence and excitement one finds on the West Side. When we came to Zabar's, I asked whether she had ever been inside the store. She shook her head.

"Then we'll go inside."

"Now? It's so crowded."

"It's always crowded," I assured her. "Don't worry. Just push your way through. I'll buy some smoked salmon for breakfast. It's Saturday night, and smoked salmon for Sunday breakfast is an article of faith with Jews. And if you enjoy food, Zabar's is like a museum of esoteric foods."

We joined the throng. I took a ticket, which would

entitle me to be served from the smoked-fish counter, but not in less than fifteen minutes. I was thinking that she would not be having breakfast with me tomorrow, unless I asked her to, then recalling Charlie's quick decision that I was in love with her. The thought made me smile—Ike Goldman in love at age seventy-eight. Old Ike Goldman. What an absolutely ridiculous proposition.

"Your whole face changes when you smile. You smile like a small boy."

"Thank you. Bless you."

"This place is wonderful, Ike. Tell me about it. What is all that stuff?"

"There, sturgeon." We slipped in front of the waiting crowd, and I explained to nettled people that it was education, not bad manners. "Herring, pickled herring, matches herring, schmaltz herring." Everyone became good natured and appreciative. "Chopped herring and chopped liver. Lox—smoked salmon. Smoked trout, smoked whitefish, smoked carp."

"Smoked carp. Wonderful," a tall blond woman said. "I never knew what that was."

A man I knew from the college, but whose name I could not recall, said, "Professor, I didn't know you were into food."

"Olives," I told Elizabeth, "green large, green small, black—they're the best. Brown and long, Greek."

"Italian," someone said.

"If you wish."

We finished the fish counter, and Elizabeth whispered, "They're not all Jewish. That woman who thanked you for the carp isn't. And look at all the black people, and those two with their collars turned, they're priests."

"Oh yes, Elizabeth, the word gets around." I steered her to the prepared-food counter, where I pointed out the barbecued chicken, boiled tongue, corned beef, lasagna, prepared pastas of three kinds, kasha-varanakas, egg rolls—to the amusement of the waiting customers as well as Elizabeth, who appeared to have lost her shyness and was actually enjoying my professorial lecture. Our tour continued, and finally we emerged with a bag of rolls, half a pound of smoked salmon, and a lump of cream cheese.

She was laughing. "I haven't laughed in weeks. Oh, I was so embarrassed. Weren't you embarrassed, Ike?"

"You spend a lifetime lecturing and nothing embarrasses you."

"That small Oriental man who was slicing the salmon—did you see the way he looked at you?"

"Ocho—old friend. He probably thought I had gone crazy."

We walked on uptown, and I asked her whether I should stop a cab and take her home.

For a long moment, she did not answer. Then she said, "I'd rather walk, if you don't mind?"

"No, I like to walk. It's my only exercise, if you can call it that. I like walking but I hate exercise." For a few blocks she was silent, and I accepted her silence. Something was happening to both of us. Finally, she said, "Ike, I think this is the best evening in my whole life."

I shook my head.

"Yes, believe me."

"If you want me to, I'll believe you. It's a good evening for me, too. It's my first date, and I'm too old for dating."

"You mean—since your wife died?"

"Yes. It's been a lonely three years. I picked you up last night on a bridge, and I don't know a thing about you. But I was married to a woman for forty years, and sometimes I feel that I didn't know very much about her. You're Elizabeth Hopper, young enough to be my daughter, and somehow, I don't want to say good night to you."

"Because I might kill myself?"

"No, I don't think you'll try it again."

"But we'll never see each other after tonight, will we," she said unhappily.

"Do you want to see me again?"

"Yes," she said without hesitation. "Yes, please."

"I bought a half pound of smoked salmon and half a dozen rolls called bialys. Have you ever tasted them?"

"Of course. I love them."

"Too much for me to eat in a week. I was sort of

hoping that I could entice you to breakfast at my apartment tomorrow."

"But you have things to do—I can't just barge into your life."

"I have nothing to do. My Sundays are days of rest, like most other days of my life—rest and boredom."

"What time?"

"About eleven."

"Oh, good. I'll go to early Mass and then I'll be there. What shall I wear?"

"No one else will be there. Come in jeans if you wish."

We walked to her home on Ninety-sixth Street, and I took her to her bare apartment, where we shared another glass of wine, served in those infamous goblets. We talked, and I learned a good deal about her. Her maiden name was Mary Elizabeth White. Until she went to college, she had been a student at a convent school, the Academy of the Sacred Heart, after which she earned her M.A. from St. Mary's in South Bend, Indiana. For eight years after that, she had worked at St. Mary's as an instructor in pastel painting. There were some relationships with various men, but nothing serious until in one of those odd accidents of life, she met Sedge Hopper. He was a large, handsome man, a great athlete with a shock of blond hair. He was dominating and used to getting what he wanted, and he worked as an investment banker, a specialist in mergers and acquisitions. I asked her whether his full name was William Sedgwick Hopper, and while she was curious to know why I asked, I brushed it off with a passing word about seeing it in the papers. Evidently she knew little more about the case than I did. "Yes," she said, "his name is William Sedgwick Hopper, but everyone called him Sedge. No one ever called him Bill or Billy.

"He thought I was beautiful—or said that he thought that. Perhaps I was pretty—prettier than I am now—but not beautiful. He said that he wanted someone unspoiled. He seemed to think that my being a student at Sacred Heart and then at St. Mary's made me into some kind of a saint. I wasn't in love with him, but my mother had begun to despair of my ever marrying, and I suppose the fact that he came from a good family, as she put it, and was a Catholic, meant a lot to her. The strange thing was that he married anyone, because he did not like women. Every woman was to him a cunt or a whore. He had been married before, but he had the marriage annulled. He boasted that it cost him ten thousand dollars. He wanted children, and I didn't become pregnant. He never forgave me for that. The first time he hit me—"

She began to cry, and I stopped her. "That's enough for tonight, Elizabeth. We'll talk about it another time—if you want to talk about it."

"I'm sorry. I mustn't dump on you like this. I don't

know why I'm telling you all this. I never told anyone else—"

"My mother used to say, 'A sorrow shared is but half a trouble, though a joy that is shared is a joy made double.' That's kind of old-fashioned, and God help you if I ever make you listen to my woes."

"I don't know why—"

"No," I said firmly. "Don't finish the thought. I'm glad you saw the two priests in Zabar's. The ecumenism of food must never be underrated. My father, when we visited New York from Oneonta, upstate, used to take my mother to Dinty Moore's, where their specialties were corned beef and gefilte fish. My mother was critical of the gefilte fish, and she gave them her own recipe, which they embraced and which brought them fame among the Jewish epicures. I will see you tomorrow. Do you remember my address?" I gave her my card, just to be sure.

She was laughing. She was actually laughing. Her face changed, and suddenly she threw her arms around me and kissed me.

I took a cab home, stuffed a pipe, and sat down in my armchair for a conversation with myself, something like: "My aged and foolish Ike—what in hell's name are you getting yourself into? You are living here alone, perfectly content—well, if not content, reasonable and thereby with endurable misery—and you can sit here in the living room, where you were never permitted to smoke, and fill the air with noxious fumes and no one gives a damn; and if you want to stay in bed for half a day, you can do that, too; and you are entangling yourself with a broken, brutalized woman, and you don't know why or where it will lead you—" At that point, I broke off the conversation. I had slept poorly the night before, and I decided that what I needed was a good night's sleep. And as for staying in bed for half a day, that had happened only once, when I had the flu.

I went to bed, took a small sleeping pill, and fell asleep almost immediately, sleeping until eight o'clock the following morning. Then I showered and shaved and set the dining-room table.

I set out to plan a Sunday date. Not that I expected to be with her the entire day, but I felt a need to suppose it might happen that way. I was never much of a lady's man, and aside from being invited to various faculty dinner parties to fill in a male seat, I had dated no woman since my wife died. Mine had been a comfortable marriage to a woman who taught mathematics at the New School and who was far more interested in cooking and being a housewife than in law.

The truth was that I wanted to be with Elizabeth the whole day. If last night had been a catharsis for Elizabeth, it was for me the best evening spent in a long time. By ten o'clock I had decided that if she loved music, we would find a concert—there are always ample concerts on a Sunday afternoon in New York—and then possibly dinner and a movie, unless she was good and tired of me by then.

I kept looking at the clock. I decided that it was not too early to telephone Charlie Brown.

He growled that it was too early. "It's Sunday," he said. "Don't you know it's Sunday?"

"Of course I know it's Sunday. That's how I knew I would find you at home in the bosom of your family," I replied mollifyingly. "I want you to do something for me."

"What? Tell me so I can go back to sleep."

"No, if you go back to sleep, you'll forget."

"OK, what can I do for you?"

"You remember that chap you spoke to me about? Harvey Goldberg in Business Administration? You said he could give me the whole story about William Sedgwick Hopper."

"Ike, what in hell have you gotten yourself into?"

"I'm not sure," I said slowly. "But if you could arrange a lunch with Goldberg tomorrow or the next day, I would be grateful."

"The woman on the bridge?"

"Yes, the woman on the bridge."

"Ike," he said, fully awake now, "this could be a scam. You've never been down the garden path."

"This is Hopper's ex-wife. It's no scam, and whatever it is, I'm involved."

"You're more than involved. Hopper is a first-class prick. You don't need Goldberg to tell you that. Just read the business section of the *Times*. I don't know whether you're in love or being taken, but don't go up against Hopper. He's poison."

"Charlie, I'm not going up against Hopper. I have no intention of going up against Hopper. But I have to know about him and what he did and how he did it. I'm no Boy Scout. I did five years in World War II. I was in the Normandy landing right up to the end."

"That was a long time ago, Ike. All right. I'll round up Goldberg, and you pick up the check."

At eleven o'clock, precisely, that Sunday morning, the doorbell buzzed. She must have been walking around outside to arrive exactly when she did, not a moment later. She was dressed in blue jeans. Her ruddy complexion needed no makeup, and the wind outside had added a blush to her cheeks. She wore a long heavy sweater over a linen shirt, and she looked younger than her forty-seven years, just as I was certain I looked older than my seventy-eight. We shook hands; neither of us tried to kiss the other, and I don't know which of the two of us was more awkward at the moment. I said something to the effect of, "Come inside and make yourself comfortable"; and she walked into the living room, facing the wide entrance to the dining room. I had laid out the salmon on a platter, flanked it with cream cheese and a basket of the hot rolls, just out of the oven a few minutes before she arrived.

"It's lovely," Elizabeth said. "And you can see the Hudson River. I could never get used to that. If I lived here, I'd just sit and stare."

"I'll get the coffee," I said. "Unless you want something first—like a glass of wine?"

"At eleven o'clock in the morning?"

No answer to that. I didn't know what came first. I wasn't used to young women at eleven in the morning. I brought out the coffee and pulled out the chair facing the window. "Sit here and you can have your fill of the river."

She sat down, smiled at me, and said that I was very sweet and very funny. I never thought of myself as being either sweet or funny. "You went to church," I said—for want of any other way to open the conversation.

"Oh, yes. I'm not a very good Catholic, but I do lean on it—and I felt so good this morning."

"Where do you work, Elizabeth?" I asked rather abruptly.

"Part-time in the shoe department at Interdale's. Women's shoes. When Sedge moved us to New York— that was three years ago, just before the annulment came—my new job at Marymount fell through. I tried to find a teaching position at Manhattanville and

Fordham and some of the smaller Catholic schools, but none of the art departments was hiring. Anyway, I was sort of going to pieces, and I was paralyzed by three months of utter depression, and that's when I signed all the papers he brought me. I would have signed anything—I was so terrified of him at that point—and all I knew was that I must do what he wanted so I would never see him again."

There were tears in her eyes now, and I switched to a discourse on smoked salmon, telling her that in Copenhagen, where I had taught a semester one summer, it was the beloved food of the whole population, and they called it lox—which I had always considered to be a Yiddish word but was actually the name for it in all the Northern countries. I piled her plate with salmon and a large lump of cream cheese, and then I spelled out my plans for the day, tentatively.

"I can't take your whole Sunday. I thought it would just be breakfast."

"Let me tell you about my Sunday," I said. "I would read the *New York Times,* which would take about three hours. Then I would have some scrambled eggs and toast. Then I would take a walk, and then I would come back here and listen to the Boston Symphony on Channel 13 and probably fall asleep. Can you imagine anything more important or exciting?"

"Ike—why?"

"If you don't stop crying, I can't tell you. A woman's tears break me up."

"I love music," she said, drying her eyes, "but I'm wearing jeans."

"Fine. Absolutely de rigueur. Now eat."

She was hungry. I watched her finish the lox and cream cheese and two bialys and two cups of coffee. There was no use lying to myself. There was something about her that absolutely fascinated me—an openness and vulnerability, and a gentle acceptance of this relationship that she, like myself, was unwilling to let go of, which left me wondering whether anyone had been kind to her since she had been here in New York. I found her very attractive physically, and I thought of myself kissing and caressing her—at the same time feeling that I, out of my own loneliness, was using her. She was intelligent, well educated, and we talked about books and art. As I was to find out, her knowledge of art and its history was encyclopedic.

The plan worked well. In the *Times* we found a string quartet offering an all-Mozart program scheduled to play in a small hall, and having a few hours to spare, we bundled up and walked across to the Metropolitan Museum of Art. We did the French Impressionists, and I got her to talk, and emerged better informed than I had been. She knew her subject. At the concert I held her hand. It was the first overt move I had made toward her, and she did not draw back. I sat through most of the concert with her small warm hand in mine, telling myself: Ike, this is sort of insane. But since I was obligated to apologize or explain to no one, I decided to hell with apologies or explanations.

The concert ended by seven, and we walked up Broadway to Romer's. It was a brisk March evening, and the wind brought color into her cheeks. She had that almost translucent skin that one finds among some Irish women, and her wide gray eyes registered her every mood and reaction. By the time our dinner was over, I had learned a good deal more about Elizabeth Hopper. It was not confessional, but in the way of having no secrets. It was in the manner of having found a life buoy—and to cling to it, she had to divest herself of every mystery. She had beautiful teeth, and when I mentioned that, in what context I don't remember, she remarked that they were implants. "It was after he discovered that I could not conceive. He went into a rage, and I lost my four front teeth."

"You lost them?"

"He knocked them out, broke them. It was a single blow to the front of my face. He was very strong from all those years of training. For the next week or two, he was very repentant. He paid for the implants—a great deal of money, and they're as good as real teeth. He was sorry. He didn't know his own strength. The few times after that when he pushed me around, he never struck my face."

"Was he drunk when he hit you?"

"No. That's the strange part of it, Ike. He never touched liquor. Bodybuilding was like a religion for him. He always said that alcohol was poison. He was crazy on the subject."

"My God, why didn't you leave him?"

"Do you know what it is like to be educated in a convent school? Your husband is the master—and Ike, I was afraid of him. He told me he would have the marriage annulled. Until then, I was to keep my mouth shut. The nuns teach you to be obedient. I thought it would take a few weeks, but it wasn't until after he joined the Wall Street firm and we moved to New York that the annulment came through. He was a strange kind of Catholic, and our parish priest had known me all my life. He had to find another priest, and that took time—and it's a complicated thing. Meanwhile, he appeared to enjoy constantly humiliating me."

"So he got the annulment, and you were divorced in the Islands?"

"Don't ask me to explain. Don't ask me how he could be a sort of demented Catholic and not believe in anything but his own rules—and his father's. His father's will said that any divorce must be locked into an annulment."

I never pressed her for details of the journey that led her to the bridge. Each humiliation tore my heart open, and the less emotion, the matter-of-fact manner that she put into the telling, made it all the worse. When they moved to New York, he bought an apartment on Park Avenue, and she moved into the apartment on the West Side. She had neither friends nor family in New York, only a few acquaintances who worked in her department at Interdale's.

When we finished dinner, it was too late for a film, and we were both tired. We had walked a great deal. When I asked her whether I should take her home, she hesitated for a long time before answering. As her assent began, I interrupted it and suggested that she come to my place, where I would start a fire in the fireplace.

"But you live in an apartment."

"An old one. And it has a fireplace. Many of the older buildings have them. I'll put you in a cab later. It's only nine-thirty."

"And you're not bored with me, Ike? We've been together all day."

"I'm not bored. Are you?"

"No, it's been a good day for me, the best. And you must call me Liz. Everyone does."

We took a cab to my apartment, and I busied myself with building a fire, while Elizabeth fixed herself at the dining-room window, overlooking the river. "I can't get enough of it. It's a whole other thing at night."

"Yes, it changes. It always changes."

"If I lived here, I'd spend my life at this window."

"Oh, Liz, I don't think so. You'd get used to it."

"No—how could I?" She came into the living room now and stood in front of the fire. "I wouldn't get used to this either, Ike." The big couch faced the fire, and she dropped onto it, stretching her legs.

"This looks like a dream," she said, "sitting here in the center of New York, in front of a fireplace, with that wonderful river out there—when did you find me on the bridge? Was it a whole lifetime ago?"

"Friday night—an old Jew driving home from a coffee klatch."

"Why do you keep referring to yourself as an old man?"

"Because I'm an old man. Seventy-nine come December, old enough to be your grandfather."

"No, no, not my grandfather. You're filled with life and warmth and compassion—and you're very wise. When you told me at dinner that a man like Sedge Hopper is not born out of a bad seed but is shaped by a society that venerates greed and power above all else, I began to understand him for the first time."

"Which does not make him any less wicked."

"But God would understand and forgive him."

I had no answer to that. I asked whether I might bring her something, some port perhaps?

"Nothing. I'm totally content—until I open my eyes and discover this is all a dream."

"Not a dream, not at all, Liz."

We sat on the couch, side by side, ten inches or so between us, talking a little but mostly staring at the fire and watching it burn down. At last, I said, "Time to go, Liz?" But the last thing in the world I wanted was for her to leave me. I felt that if she did, the past three days would disappear in a puff of smoke.

She didn't answer my question.

"It's almost eleven."

"My shift begins at two P.M. and I work until nine."

"Still, you have to go home!"

"Why?" Now she spoke like a little child, pleadingly. "Why do I have to go home, Ike? I don't want to go back to that dreadful apartment. Why can't I sleep in your son's room where I slept the first night?" Then the boldness of her request overcame her and she leaped to her feet, shaking her head. "No, I'm making a fool of myself! What an awful thing to ask you! She strode out of the room to the entry, and when I followed her, she was struggling into her long sweater.

"Liz," I said gently, grasping her by the arms, "let go of the sweater. Of course you can stay over. Please.

Now come sit down again and we'll let the fire burn out."

She allowed herself to be led back to the sofa. "I shouldn't have asked you. I wasn't making a pass, Ike, believe me, please. I don't want to use you or take advantage of your kindness. It would be better if you let me go home."

"No, I'm afraid you're trapped, Liz. I'll sleep better if I know you're in the next room."

"Because you still think I'll kill myself? No, Ike, that's over. Don't you understand? You came by on the bridge because it was not my time to die. You were sent. I know you don't believe that, but I do; and it's no excuse for me to act like a spoiled child. I'm a grown woman of forty-seven years, and I'll go home and I'll be all right."

"Yes, of course. And I'm an old man of seventy-eight years, and I care for you whether I was sent there or not. I want you to stay over—let's say for my sake. I want to make breakfast for you in the morning. I want to know that you'll be here when I wake up. I'm very seriously asking you to stay."

"Why, Ike?"

"Because you brought me a few days of happiness. Isn't that enough?"

"Thank you, Ike. I want to stay."

I took the sweater and put it back in the closet.

Elizabeth went to the couch and stared at the glowing coals of the fire. I put Bach's *Air on the G String* on the stereo, then sat with her on the couch, again with a space between us, watching her. I must have dozed.

"Midnight, Ike," she said. The fire was out.

I'm not a good night person. Elizabeth stood up and reached out a hand to help me to my feet. "Stiff and old," I said. She shook her head.

"Do you need anything?" I asked. "Pajamas?"

"No, not a thing. You're very tall. I would be lost in your pajamas." At the door to my son's room, she reached out a hand to me and kissed me on my cheek. "Good night, Ike. Bless you."

Sometime that night, I suppose close to four o'clock in the morning, I awakened, and there was Elizabeth, in bed with me and sound asleep. She must have crawled in during the night, very quietly and without waking me. I didn't wake her, and when I awoke again, past nine, she was up and dressed, and the aroma of fresh coffee drifted out of the kitchen.

She greeted me again with a soft kiss, on my lips this time, informing me that she must get home, change her clothes, and be off to work.

"I have a cook in twice a week, and this is her night. Will you come for a nice, civilized dinner, just the two of us?"

"Ike, you will be so tired of me."

"But you'll come?"

"Of course I will. What time?"

"Around six-thirty or so."

There was no artifice to her. What was there, you saw—no hint of coyness or pretense. She kissed me again as she departed, leaving me to wonder who was who in this curious relationship that I had stepped into so casually—whether she was groping for a father or shelter or simply someone who treated her as a decent and desirable human being. That she might have fallen in love with an old teacher crossed my mind, but I dropped it immediately, examining myself in the entryway mirror and critically observing the tall, skinny, elderly professorial type—a long lean face, which I had always considered less than attractive, and a decent head of hair that was mostly white. As for my falling in love—well, romantic love was something I had always considered to be an illusion that poured money into the entertainment industry, only a small step above virtual reality.

CHAPTER THREE

The Price

THE TELEPHONE RANG. It was Charlie Brown. "Believe it or not," he said, "Harvey Goldberg is delighted. He has secret aspirations for writing a book, with you as coauthor, on the subject of greed as a social force in America. He is free for lunch today, if you choose, or he'll make himself free on any other day you select. I think you should take him up on it."

"Today will be fine," I agreed.

"Twelve-thirty? Same place?"

"I'll be there."

Harvey Goldberg was a fat, jovial man, who wore pince-nez glasses and combed his thin hair across the top of his balding head. When he appeared as a business or market expert on television programs, he wore a hairpiece, but in his day-to-day lecturing, he was content with his natural hair. He chewed nicotine gum to break himself of his cigarette habit, and while he admitted his continuing addiction, he felt that it got him through the day at Columbia. I had never met him before, but then Columbia is a very large university.

Goldberg ordered a steak and fried potatoes, voicing his contempt for all dietary discoveries, and then asked me whether Charlie had told me about his idea for the book on greed, and what did I think about it?

"It's a fascinating notion," I said.

"Good. We'll talk about it another time. Charlie tells me you're squiring William Sedgwick Hopper's divorced wife."

I looked daggers at Charlie, who shrugged and said, "Harvey won't spread it."

"My lips are locked," Goldberg concurred. "I'm sixty, Ike—you don't mind if I call you Ike? Charlie says you prefer it—and I've been divorced seven years. I have a young lady of forty who's talking marriage. I understand you're a widower, Ike. How old are you, if I may ask? Sixty-eight, sixty-nine?"

"Seventy-nine, come December."

"Statistically, marriage adds eight years to your life."

Charlie tried to remedy things by reminding Goldberg that we were there to talk about Hopper.

"He was once the 'Golden Boy' of American athletics, two Olympic gold medals, but now he's a first-class, unredeemable prick. His wife had him arrested once—if you can believe the *Post*—the third time he beat her up, but she wouldn't press charges. Garson, Weeds and Anderson took him in as a portfolio manager based on his reputation. They wanted the name. He's smart the way a crook is smart. He was trading for a number of accounts, one of which was his own, and he was good. Where there were profits, he shifted them into his own account. Where there were losses, he transferred them elsewhere. I'm simplifying it; it's far more complex than this. It took three years for him to be caught, and he's into the firm for fifteen million— but the money sits in the house. He's rich enough not to need it, and they don't know how to proceed or whether they have enough evidence to put him down. In some ways, it's a classic scam. They suspended his trading, but he still keeps his office there; and they're very careful about what they give out to the press. If you read the stories in the *Times* and the *Wall Street Journal,* you'd still have a hard time figuring out what, if anything, he did that was illegal. If the money's missing, it's one thing, but the money's still there—in the firm. I had a talk with Jim Weeds about it. Weeds is worried about the face of the firm. It's not the biggest outfit on Wall Street, and fifteen mil is still a lot of money."

"Oh, I believe," I told her, "on and off—I just don't admire the way He runs things."

"He doesn't run things. He leaves it up to that wretched lot they call cops and judges."

"Spoken like a valid public defender. Do we have white wine?"

"A couple of bottles. I'll put one in the fridge."

I admit I was nervous waiting for Elizabeth to appear; the scene on the bridge would not leave me. Grateful that it was another cold evening, I had built a fire—the second time I used the fireplace that winter. At six-twenty, the doorbell rang, and there was Elizabeth, her face flushed, wearing a pleated skirt, moccasin-style shoes, and wrapped in the big taupe sweater.

"Oh, Ike," she exclaimed, "I'm so glad to be here. I took off from work early and walked all the way from home." She solved my problem of how to greet her by throwing her arms around me and embracing me, and I found myself kissing her. She didn't draw away, and I took her sweater and led her to the fireplace.

"That wonderful fireplace," she said.

"White wine?"

"Sure."

"It's a long walk from Ninety-sixth Street."

"A mile or so—nothing really."

Sarah brought in two glasses of wine, and I introduced Liz and Sarah to each other, explaining that Sarah was one of my best students.

"Yes, in contract law," Sarah said, laughing. "And I end up being a public defender."

Dinner went well. Liz loved the shrimp and ate heartily and finished the fruit tart to the last crumb. I very hesitantly asked her what she weighed, and she replied that the last time she had weighed herself, it was one hundred and ten; and then she asked me why I was so uneasy about a personal question.

"It's just—well, I don't know. You don't ask a woman what she weighs."

"I have no secrets from you, Ike. I never will."

Before leaving, Sarah took me aside and whispered, "She's all right, Ike. She's a good one."

"I think so."

"Don't chase her away."

"Not if I can help it."

After Sarah left, Liz and I had coffee in front of the fire. I told Liz that Sarah liked her.

"And you have great respect for Sarah, so I'm glad."

"She was one of my best students and she's a hell of a lawyer."

"Then why does she have to work at night?"

"Partly because public defenders are underpaid— like so many people today—and I think, because she likes me."

Liz nodded. "I can understand that."

"You know, Liz, those agreements you signed when

you were so depressed—they're all signed under duress. They wouldn't stand up in court. William Hopper is a millionaire many times over."

She was silent for a few minutes, and then she said, "Ike, I want nothing from Mr. Hopper, only to forget that he exists." Then, again, we sat in silence for a while, until Liz said, "Ike, last night I did something— oh, I don't know how to explain it, except that I had a nightmare of sorts about Sedge, and I was frightened, and I crawled into bed with you. I didn't want to awaken you but just to feel you there, and you reached out and put your arm around me without waking. I fell asleep like a child, and in the morning, I slipped away very quietly—"

"I know."

"And you never said a word?"

I nodded.

"I love you, Ike."

I thought about that for a while and then said, gently, "Liz, my dear, you've been through all kinds of hell. I reached out a hand to you. I'm an old man, and you're a lovely young woman. What can I offer you?"

"You gave me life and hope. You must care for me a little."

"More than a little—a great deal more."

"And you're not an old man, Ike. If age is the accumulation of a knowledge of pain and wickedness, then I'm older than you'll ever be. They say a woman who has just been divorced is not to be believed in her reactions, but I never really knew Sedge Hopper and I knew you from the first day. I know you ask yourself, Who is she?—this Elizabeth Hopper who stayed for years with a man who brutalized her and degraded her. But thousands of women remain with men who brutalize them. You can't know what it is to spend fourteen years—your growing-up years—attending a convent school, to be taught to love, honor, and obey the man who will be your husband. But now I'm breaking all those rules. I love you. I never thought I could say that."

This was not a conversation that moved back and forth, like the dialogue in a play. I had no immediate answers for Liz, but I moved close to her and put my arm around her, and she laid her head on my shoulder. Then we sat quietly and watched the fire burn down to coals. For me, the closeness and warmth of her body were like a benediction. Love is a peculiar thing, and there is little love in what goes for it on the screen and in books, which is mostly a tearing apart of flesh and soul. I looked into myself for some truth, and that's the most difficult of all things—it's so much easier to lie to yourself than to others. And if the comfort and completeness I felt with Liz pressed up against my body was love, then I loved her; and at least I knew one thing with certainty, that I never wanted her to leave me.

"The fire is almost out," Liz said. "Do you have more wood, Ike?"

"Everything is virtual reality today, Liz. That's not wood but some kind of pressed stuff that I bought in the hardware store. No more now, but tomorrow I'll buy some."

"You're real, Ike. I'm real."

"Will you come to bed with me, Liz?"

"Yes," she said simply.

That night, I made no effort to make love to Elizabeth. That was still in the future, and in all truth, I was afraid. Lena and I had used separate rooms for the last few years of her life. She was a sick woman who fought desperately to live, and I had existed as a monk of sorts, successfully denying any libido. But Liz curled up against me, her head on my chest, kissing me gently and asking for nothing more. That way, she fell asleep. My own sleeping was less successful, but eventually I dozed off and slept.

In the morning I awakened about eight, and Liz was gone from the bed, and there were sounds and coffee smells from the kitchen. When I had showered and dressed and joined her, there was a royal breakfast of juice and cereal and eggs and yogurt and toast, and we sat over breakfast eating and talking until suddenly she realized that she had to go to work and dashed off with a hug and a kiss.

For the next five weeks, we lived together. Bit by bit,

she brought her clothes to my apartment, and finally a suitcase packed with what was left. We never discussed this arrangement; it happened because we both wanted it to happen. After a month, I persuaded her to give up her apartment and to have the bit of mail she received forwarded to my address. When Sarah was not there, Liz did the cooking. She was a good cook, and our life settled into the pattern of an old married couple, yet newly married enough for both of us to be delighted with each other. My son's room became her room, and one day I bought her a gift of an easel and paper and pastel crayons, which delighted her.

And I made love to her, hesitantly at first, and then with wonder and absolute delight. We learned each other, and I found that love and the ability to make love was not a matter of chronology. Oh, I had my guilt that this was something I had never known before, guilt about the age difference, guilt about the passion of her love for me, guilt about the sense that I was taking advantage of her. Liz took a brown paper bag and printed on it: THIS IS A GUILT RECEPTACLE. BREATHE INTO IT SLOWLY, FOUR TIMES. THEN CLOSE IT AND YOUR GUILTS WILL VANISH.

As I watched the change in her—the awakening of a bright and lovely spirit—my own happiness responded. I tried to persuade her to give up her job, but she refused, declaring that she needed money of her own for the day when I tossed her back into the street—

a bit of bitter humor that I did not take well. Weekends we explored the city on foot, went to the museums, to concerts, and to the theater. And once she said, "I'm so happy, Ike, that I'm frightened. I'm really terrified that this will end."

"All things end, Liz—but not for a long time."

"What will I do if anything happens to you?"

"Nothing will happen to me. I'm as healthy as an ox."

She studied me for a long moment, her wide gray eyes fixed on my face, and then she said, "I take from you, Ike. What do I give you?"

"Life," I replied.

"Oh, come on. You gave it to me. You saved my life."

"If I did save your life, my dear, I saved the life of a frightened, broken woman. I took you home with me because I didn't know what else to do with you."

"And you were afraid I would kill myself, left alone. And then you gave me a home and protection and love. But what did I give you, Ike?"

"I watched you unfold. I watched you come alive, and I found a wonderful woman, someone who loved me. I didn't know what love was; it's a cheap word that's everywhere. I found someone who became a part of me, someone I could talk to about anything; and as you unfolded, I unfolded. Do you understand that, Liz?"

"I think I do."

"Everything changed. I began to see things with your eyes, with a kind of innocence that I had always rejected."

"Ike," she whispered, "you're not just saying that?"

"Believe me, Liz. I love you. Perhaps I have only a few years left, but if I can spend them with you—well, that's enough. I'm very lucky. I would ask for no more than that. If you left me—"

"I'll never leave you, Ike."

I have a large library, a whole wall of the living room covered with the acquisitions of a lifetime; law books, court records, history, philosophy, and novels. When my son married, he took his books with him, but I still had *Tom Sawyer* and *Huckleberry Finn* and *Treasure Island* from my age-ten-to-twelve time and a hundred other novels that I kept and treasured. Books that I did not feel deserved keeping, I would give away to whatever charity accepted books, but each of them was weighed and judged before I parted with it. I never throw away a book; such an action rates high on my catalog of sins.

Liz's response to this wall of books was sheer delight and chaotic curiosity. Whenever she worked a late shift at the store, and a short one at that, there was time for reading. I have thanked whatever gods may be for my good eyesight and for my ability to read for hours, and very often we would both curl up with a book, sometimes in the early hours, sometimes in the evening. I never attempted to direct her reading or to recommend a book. In some ways, she was better educated than I was; but she was more hungry than I for words and ideas, and she had told me that aside from the few books she'd brought into her marriage home, there were no books in the Hopper house, except for a few oversized coffee-table tomes on hunting.

One evening, when each of us sat with a book, I asked her what she was reading.

"Daniel Berrigan," she replied, holding up the book. "It's called *No Bars to Manhood.*"

I nodded.

"Have you read it?" she asked me.

"Yes—but that was a long time ago, perhaps twenty-five years. He's a Jesuit priest who was involved in the peace movement against the Vietnam War."

"I'm not reading him because he's a priest."

"I didn't say that."

"But you were thinking it."

"Possibly," I admitted. "I was also involved in the peace movement at that time."

"Perhaps I was reading it because he was a priest. It came out during my last year in high school. The nuns wouldn't allow us to even discuss Father Berrigan, and when I saw it here—"

"For heaven's sake, you don't have to apologize for anything you read!"

"Ike—Ike, I am not apologizing, only explaining—but when it comes to anything about you being a Jew and me being a Catholic, you shy away."

"I don't shy away," I objected. "We are what we are, and we love each other. It is 1996."

"But my dear, dear Ike, we are because I am a Catholic and you are a Jew. That's why we know each other so well. May I read something to you?"

"Of course."

"This was during the war, Ike, and Father Berrigan wrote, 'I seek so simple a thing as—sanity. For I confess to you that I regard these people, who are my people, with a growing horror, this believing nation that sounds its prayers as it goes about the task of Cain.'" She glanced up at me. "Do you understand, Ike?"

"I think so," I admitted uncertainly.

"Ike, you gave me something—Father Berrigan calls it sanity. You took me by the hand and led me from death to life. Sedge Hopper is a Catholic, and I have been struggling with that. Then I began to read this book, and I understand so much. I will always be a Catholic and you will always be a Jew. And it will never matter as something between us because there is nothing separating us."

I thought I understood her, but I was not sure. I knew many Catholics, but never one who spoke about his or her religion. The next day, when Liz was at work, I read through the Berrigan book. I spoke to Charlie

Brown, who is Catholic, but he shied away from anything deeper than the surface. The subject made him
uncomfortable.

Liz was changing, emerging, becoming stronger.
My role as a father figure, if indeed it had ever existed,
was gone. Bit by bit, she was taking hold of my life, seeing to it that I ate properly, dragging me out for long
walks in any and every kind of weather. At the same
time, she and Sarah Morton were becoming close
friends.

She said that she wanted to go to a synagogue;
and when I told her that I had not set foot in a synagogue since age thirteen, she answered, "That's your
problem, Ike. Mine is to know all I can about you. If
you will take me to a synagogue, I will take you to
Sunday Mass."

We went one Friday evening, walking down to the
Free Synagogue on Sixty-eighth Street. I had made the
mistake of telling her that observant Jews do not ride
on the Sabbath, and she decided that for once in my
life, I would be an observant Jew. The Mass followed
two days later. My feet still ached, but fortunately the
church was much closer to 115th Street. Yet nothing
was done with stress; I had only to look at her and then
ask myself: Why not?

For the first two weeks we slept together, she had
frightening nightmares. She would awaken sobbing
and crawl into my arms, but in time they became fewer

and less frequent. She spoke a great deal about her life, about attending a strict convent school for so many years and laughing good-naturedly about some of the archaic Victorian "guidelines of ladylike deportment" the nuns taught her. But instead of a cold holding back, convent or no, she entered into sex with a passion that was almost too much for me. Once, on a Sunday afternoon, when we stretched out on my bed after a walk, I protested that it was sinful to do this in daylight.

"Oh, Ike," she said, laughing, "you have the strangest catalog of sins that are not sinful. Your Puritan ancestors—"

"I have no Puritan ancestors. I'm Jewish."

"Doesn't matter. You know, the Indians who helped them survive loved to have sex on a nearby hillside in the afternoon sun. The Puritans decided it was an affront to God, and slaughtered them."

"Did you learn that in the convent?"

"No. Read it somewhere. And you've never done anything sinful."

She kissed me, and that finished my argument. She changed, she flowered; and I was an old man falling hopelessly in love. But there was one thing she never spoke of—her life with her one-time husband. Aside from telling about her teeth being broken, she said almost nothing about her life with him. And then, one evening, the telephone rang and a voice announced that it was William Sedgwick Hopper, and that he would like to speak to Mrs. Hopper. I held my hand over the phone and called to Liz, "It's your ex-husband. He wants to talk. You don't have to. I'll tell him to buzz off and forget it."

Liz stood facing me, her lips tight, a look in her eyes I had never seen before. A long moment passed before she spoke. "No, Ike. I'll talk to him. I'll take it in the kitchen." And with that, she walked into the kitchen, closing the door behind her. When I heard her say hello, I put the phone back in its cradle. But closed door or not, her voice came through, a raging voice that I would have believed Elizabeth incapable of. "You bastard!" she shouted. "You rotten, unspeakable bastard! How dare you call me here—or anywhere else! Don't you ever call me again! Ever! Ever, do you understand?" Then there was a long moment of silence, and then again, Liz's raging voice, "Do you know what my response is to that? Fuck off, you miserable creep!" Perhaps a minute passed before Liz flung open the kitchen door and strode into the dining room, her arms flung wide.

"Look at me, Ike! Just look at me!"

"What did he want?"

"He wanted the gold bracelet. Can you imagine! He called to tell me that he intended to take action to get the bracelet, and that he had spoken to his attorney. Do you know what I said?"

"I heard you through the door. I'm proud of you."

"Proud of me? Why, Ike? My behavior was deplorable. After all, he once was my husband."

"Your response was magnificent, and we'll leave it right there."

She was laughing now. "Do you believe it, Ike? Can you believe me? I never used that word before, never in my whole life! I know what Mom would have said. She would have said, 'Now you've learned the Irish language!' I said it—and I am Irish. Don't you think that's very remarkable, Ike?"

"Very remarkable," I managed.

Liz paused, a long, long moment then. When she spoke, her voice was low and even. "You know, Ike, it was Don Byrne who decided that profanity was the Irish language. Maybe because the Irish were brutalized for seven hundred years. You can get over that, but not easily.

"I'm not the woman you found on the bridge, or the woman Sedge Hopper knew. She died on the bridge that night. You healed me—but for what? I learned to hate. God forgive me, I hate Sedge Hopper with all my heart and soul. I never knew there were such thoughts inside of me. I know it's sinful and it's wrong, but I wish him dead. I wish him to burn in hell. I hate his guts. I hate his beautiful blond hair, his beautiful athletic body, his foul, vicious tongue, his sick, rotten mind.

And now that you know what is inside of me, you can stop loving me."

"Why, Liz? Why should I stop loving you?"

"Because hatred is wrong and destructive. Tomorrow, I'll confess. I'll tell Father O'Donnell what I feel— but I don't think those thoughts will leave me. I wasn't born to sell shoes, Ike. I know what I want to do now. I want to help other battered women. If it means going to school again, I'll do that. Do you know how it feels, Ike, to have your arm twisted until it breaks, to hide in your room with black eyes and a fractured jaw, to plead with someone to stop beating you?" Her eyes bored into me.

"Liz," I said, "stop living that. It's over. You'll never see Sedge Hopper again. I love you for what you are. If you want to be a social worker, that's wonderful. As for your thoughts—they're normal. What else could you feel? It's been bottled up inside of you. Thank God it's out."

"Do you believe that, Ike?"

"With all my heart. Now let's talk about something else."

She threw her arms around me, kissed me. "Dear, dear darling Ike—do you see what you did for me? You made me a person!"

"You've always been a person—a good, beautiful person."

"But Ike," she said, her tone suddenly changing, "how did he find me? How did he get this phone number?" She drew back now.

"That's simple, Liz. He called your old number, and the recording gave him my number."

"Can he find me here? Does he know where we live?"

"Liz, what's the difference? There's nothing to be afraid of."

"No! No, no, no!" She faced me, erect and serious. "I will never be afraid of him again. I was always afraid of him, of his words and his fists and his guns, but no more. I will never be afraid of him—no, Ike, never. And you will be there for me, always."

"Always," I agreed.

Hopper did not call again, and as for his attorney, we never received even a letter. It would have been an easy matter for him to have found out where we lived. Evidently he'd given up his battle for the gold bracelet. Liz settled in. This was her home now, and she cherished every bit of the apartment. She consulted with Sarah Morton on each meal, did the shopping, and insisted on paying for the food she bought. When I argued that she would be wiser to put her small wages in the bank, she rejected the notion. When I mentioned that she was my guest, she opposed the idea indignantly. "I don't pay rent, and you've given me more than I ever dreamed of. I love you, Ike. If I had a million dollars, I would give it to you."

Liz was one of those women who could turn her hand to almost anything. She restored order to a house that had not known order for years. She sewed back the buttons I had lost, did my washing, insisted that the laundry I used could not iron my shirts properly and ironed them herself. She was consumed with new energy that appeared to be boundless.

We began to invite my friends to dinner. There was general approval of Liz and, in some cases, envy. Charlie Brown advised me, "Marry her, Ike, while she's still under the influence of whatever you feed her. Otherwise, she'll wake up someday and ask herself what she's doing in bed with an old fart like you."

When I repeated this to Liz, she looked at me quizzically and said, "What did you tell him?"

"All in good time."

"You'd have to ask me first."

"I'm too old."

"What a cop-out!" she exclaimed. It was the first time I had seen even a touch of anger toward me in Liz.

"All right. Elizabeth Hopper, will you marry me?"

"Yes. Right now. I'll take the day off work."

"It's not practical today. How about next week?"

"OK. Next week."

"I'm Jewish and you're Catholic. Does that make any difference?"

"Not to me. Does it make any difference to you?"

"Good heavens, no," I said. "How shall we do it?"

She threw her arms around me and kissed me. "Any way you like, City Hall or a rabbi or a priest— well, perhaps not a priest. How about a judge? You know enough judges."

"Consider it done," I said.

I was tired that Friday evening, and at nine o'clock, I told Liz that I was going to bed.

"But it's only nine!" She was alive, alert, glowing— a new Liz, a different Liz—as if our discussion of marriage had cut the last bit of bondage that had tied her to William Sedgwick Hopper. Her cheeks were flushed, and at that moment I thought her totally beautiful.

"I am old."

Her eyes flashed with annoyance. "Don't say that— not ever again! You are not old. You're the youngest man I ever knew. When I was twenty, I often went to bed at nine. You have a right to be tired at any age, so go to bed and rest. Myself, I can't sleep. I'm going out for a walk."

"Now? Alone? It's dark."

"I don't care. I'll be all right, Ike. I'm just bursting, and I have to walk."

"I'll go with you," I said.

"No, no. I want to be alone and breathe and think. Go to bed, and I'll crawl in with you the moment I'm back."

I let her have her way. Disagreements with Liz were infrequent, but I always let her have her way. There would be no memories of Hopper in our relationship. Liz put on a heavy sweater and left, with a hug and a kiss that did not lessen my anxieties. I undressed and went to bed. I decided that I would not sleep until she returned, but I must have dozed because the next thing I remember was Liz crawling into bed with me, her cold feet tangled with mine and her arms around me. I didn't look at our bedroom clock or know what time it was.

Since I'd met her, Liz had not missed a Sunday morning Mass. We talked a good deal about her Catholicism and my Judaism. When I said that I was a Jew without religion, she protested that I was a totally religious man. "I don't go to confession," she said, "and I don't live by the pope's every dictum. I do go to Mass and I receive Communion. I try to live decently and I believe in God."

This Sunday morning—just over two months after the incident on the bridge—at eight o'clock, with Liz at church for the early Mass, I opened my *New York Times*. There is a feeling in a certain circle of New Yorkers that if one does not dedicate himself to the Sunday *Times*, one will be lost to the flow of life. I know people who have not lived in the city for years, yet for whom the Sunday *Times* continues to be scripture. Whether anyone has either the time or the inclination to read the entire enormous paper, I don't know. I start with the news section, followed by the "Week in Review," the magazine, and the book section—and rarely go any further. On this Sunday, the news section had a left-hand two-column article headed: MYSTERIOUS DEATH OF AN OLYMPIC ATHLETE, and reading on, I learned that William Sedgwick Hopper had been found dead at his desk after midnight Saturday morning, with a bullet hole in the back of his head. The details were sketchy, the police evidently unwilling to provide much information at this time, and the partners of the firm he worked for equally unwilling to discuss the case. There was some reprise of the investigation of Hopper's trading methods and some background of his history as an Olympic gold-medal winner but no mention of his divorce, or of Elizabeth— for which I was grateful.

I must admit that I was both relieved and satisfied that a brute had met his just deserts. I had never met the man, but out of Liz's fragmentary references to her experiences, I had a fairly full picture of him. I re- minded myself not to share my reaction with Liz when she returned from church, since she was so wedded to her belief that vengeance belonged to God and only to God and that even a glint of satisfaction on my part would have disturbed her.

When she returned from Mass, glowing from her walk, radiant as she usually was on a Sunday morning,

I showed her the paper. She said nothing as she read the story, but the happiness washed out of her.

"Poor man," she said softly.

I couldn't help asking, "Why? Why poor man?"

"Because he never had a chance to live or to know himself."

There was a great deal I could have said in response to that, but I swallowed my thoughts and said only that at least he would bother her no more.

"I never really wanted him dead. I always hoped he might change."

"Such men never change, Liz."

She simply shook her head, and I had a new insight into the mind of this woman whom I had met by chance and who had changed the course of my life. For the rest of that Sunday, she made no reference to Hopper's death—nor did I refer to the subject. That evening, back at my apartment—she was in no mood for entertainment—there were calls from both Charlie Brown and Harvey Goldberg, whom I had seen several times since our first luncheon and whom we now watched whenever he appeared on one of the networks to tell us whether the economy was going straight to the stars or straight to hell. Charlie shared my satisfaction, and Harvey Goldberg informed me that Elizabeth had a great opportunity for a piece of the decedent's estate. I took both calls in the bedroom, out of Liz's hearing, and reminded Goldberg that I was an expert in contract law and that Liz would be enraged at even the suggestion.

I had replenished my fire-log supply, and as we sat in front of the fireplace that evening, I said to Liz, "I have been thinking of asking Rena Nussbaum—she sits on the State Supreme Court—to perform the wedding ceremony. I thought you might enjoy having a woman marry us. It could be a week from today, here at the apartment, just a few close friends, about ten or twelve couples, and we could have a little party, champagne and sandwiches. I'll get Zabar's to put together one of their big sandwich trays—or maybe I should have the whole thing catered. I want to have Sarah here as a guest."

"Yes—it would be nice to have a woman marry us. I feel so odd—I don't have anyone to invite. I can't ask people to come from Boston. But, Ike, let's postpone it for another week—I feel strange about it coming so close after Sedge's death."

"If you wish. It's only a ceremony."

"It's more than that for me," Liz said. "And perhaps you can find a rabbi or I can find a priest who will marry us. It would be a bit nicer than a judge—I mean for me."

"Sure. I won't love you any less next week."

That was Sunday.

That night, with Liz sleeping soundly, curled up against me, my own sleep would not come. Occasionally, when sleep defied me, I took a mild sleeping pill, Temazepam in the amount of twenty milligrams. I thought of taking one then, but I knew that if I moved, it would awaken Liz—so I chose to lie there quietly and be a victim of my thoughts. I was asking myself, who was Elizabeth Hopper? With all our days together, how much did I know about her? This waif—as much as I disliked the word—had entered my life out of nowhere, a woman on a bridge, measuring the distance to death; and now I had proposed marriage to her, a woman thirty years younger than I.

A few weeks ago, on a sunny Sunday afternoon when we were walking on a crowded Fifth Avenue, something happened that was so very much Elizabeth. A little boy, perhaps five years old, had been separated from his mother and stood terrified and weeping in a jungle of legs that passed him by as if he didn't exist. Without hesitating, Liz scooped him up in her arms and handed him to me. "Hold him high, Ike. You're very tall. Hold him high." And then, "Here he is! Where's Mother?"

His panic-stricken mother appeared in a moment, shouldering her way through the crowded street, taking her child, and thanking us and blessing us.

As Sarah said after meeting Liz a few times, "What you see is what you get. There's nothing hidden inside. Those are the women who suffer most."

Liz loved children, with the kind of deep, painful

love many barren women carry. After the incident on Fifth Avenue, we had talked about it; and as much as I dreaded the thought of raising another child at my age, I found myself suggesting that when we married, we might adopt a child.

"Ike, would you? Really, would you?"

Trapped, I said something to the effect that we would have to think about it carefully beforehand.

"Of course."

"It's not easy, Liz."

"They have healthy children for adoption in Russia and especially in Romania. I read about it, Ike."

"Well—I suppose we might try. I'm not young, you know—"

"Ike, you're the youngest and best man in the whole world. And I would do everything."

And now I had decided who would perform the wedding. Finally, I slept.

Three days later, Wednesday morning, while we were having breakfast, the doorbell rang. I opened the door for two men, one tall, thin, and balding and the other younger and carrottopped. The older man introduced himself as Detective Sergeant Hull and the younger man as Detective Flannery. Both of them showed me their badges, and Hull asked whether I was Professor Isaac Goldman.

"Only emeritus," I replied. "What can I do for you gentlemen?"

"Can we step inside, Professor?"

"Of course. What brings you here?"

Liz was standing in the opening between the entry-way and the dining room.

"I have a search warrant for your apartment."

"What?"

"A search warrant, sir." He handed me a folded sheaf of paper, and I opened it and saw the signature of Judge Lyman Ferguson. I knew Ferguson; I had met him several times. "You will note, Professor, that it includes your apartment as well as Mrs. Elizabeth Hopper's apartment on Ninety-sixth Street. She vacated those premises some weeks ago."

"Why on God's earth would Lyman Ferguson sign a search warrant for my apartment? He could have called me. What is all this about?"

Liz asked them to step into the living room.

"I suppose it's the death of Mr. Hopper," I said. "But what on earth are you looking for here?"

"Well, sir, you can make it easy for us. Do you have a gun?"

I went over to Liz and put my arm around her and said softly, "It's all right, baby." And then to Hull, "Yes. I have a small Colt twenty-two. It's registered and I have a permit for it."

"Would you show us where you keep it?"

I nodded. "If you'll follow me." I led them into my bedroom, where we had an eighteenth-century highboy. At the top were four small drawers, which I never opened. They were within reach, but only by standing on my toes could I see into them. In them, I kept Lena's wedding ring, a few pieces of her jewelry, and the gun and permit. I had bought the gun more than twenty years ago, had never carried it or fired it—all of which I explained to the two detectives. Buying it was an impulse of the moment when the neighborhood around Columbia University began to change for the worse. As a matter of fact, I hated guns, having had an intimate acquaintance with them during World War II.

The drawer where I had kept the gun was empty, except for a sheet of paper, which was the permit. I took it out and handed it to Hull. "I'm sure I kept it in that drawer," I said, "but I don't trust my memory that much. I'll try the others."

I went through the other three drawers. They were empty. The wedding ring was gone, along with Lena's other jewelry. Liz was watching all this, her face taut and frightened.

"Well, I've been robbed. The gun is gone and my wife's jewelry with it."

"Your wife died three years ago, Professor." They appeared to know a lot about me. "When you put her jewelry in there, did you open the drawer where you say you kept the gun?" Hull asked.

"No. I knew where I put it. I wasn't interested in the gun."

"Then if you were robbed, it was during the past three years?"

"I suppose so."

"And you never reported the robbery?" Hull demanded. "You know the law."

"Because I didn't know it had taken place," I said.

"You're a lawyer, Professor, so I presume you know you don't have to answer any of my questions?"

"I know that, and at this point I don't intend to. Do you want to continue your search?"

"I'd like to look into those drawers."

"Go ahead."

Hull was tall enough to see what the drawers contained. They were empty. He pointed to a gold chain bracelet on Liz's dressing table. "Was that your wife's?"

"No, and that's the last question I intend to answer."

"OK. We'll continue our search. We'll try not to upset things. If you and your friend would stay in the living room, it will only take about an hour."

"Go ahead," I agreed.

It took about an hour, as he said, and Liz and I sat and waited. She asked me what it was all about and what it meant, and all I could tell her was that it had something to do with Hopper's murder.

"But they don't think you killed him, Ike? Don't they understand that a man like you could not kill anyone? You're the kindest, most gentle man I ever knew, and anyway, we were together all night Friday when he was killed. We had dinner together and we slept together. So how could you have anything to do with a murder that took place—when was it? What time?"

"Sometime after the office closed, as much as I know. The *Times* said they discovered him after midnight. No, darling—there's no way they can incriminate me, and I'm not worried about it. It's a police procedure, and they have to do it by the book."

"But it makes no sense."

"A lot of things make no sense."

"I have to call the store. I'll be late for work."

"Call them. Use the phone in the kitchen. You might as well tell them that you won't be in today. Tell them you're ill."

Liz made the call, and then came back and told me that it was so hard to speak that they immediately believed her. "I hate to lie. You know I came to New York because I had been promised a job at Marymount, and I still had hopes that it might come through in September. They like me at the store, and I never told them I might quit in September. But, with all this happening—it will be in the papers, won't it, Ike?"

"It has nothing to do with you or your character."

"Will we still have the wedding next week?"

"We certainly will. The whole thing is ridiculous."

But it was not ridiculous when they finished their search—evidently finding what they were looking for. Flannery had a lipstick in his hand, and he showed it to Liz. "Is this yours?"

"We found it in the smaller bedroom. Do you have another?" Hull said.

"Yes," she whispered. "I carry one in my bag."

"The same?" He looked at the lipstick closely. "Devlon Autumn?"

"Yes."

"Would you show me your purse?"

Liz looked at me, and I nodded. Her purse was in the entryway. She went for it, then handed it to Flannery.

"Would you take out the lipstick?"

"Hold on," I said to Liz.

"If you will look at the search warrant," Hull said, "you will see that it includes the apartment and all contents."

"Give it to him," I said to her. "It makes no difference."

She opened her purse, found the lipstick, and handed it to Flannery, who put both lipsticks in a plastic bag.

"Would you stand up, please, Mrs. Hopper," Hull said.

"Why?" I demanded, standing myself now, angry

and frustrated. "What in hell has this got to do with her?"

"Please stand up, Mrs. Hopper," he repeated.

Liz rose facing him.

"Elizabeth Hopper," he said, "I am arresting you for the murder of William Sedgwick Hopper. I am going to read you your rights. You have the right to remain silent. Anything you say can and will be used against you in a court of law. You have the right to have an attorney present during questioning. If you cannot afford an attorney, one will be appointed for you. Do you understand this?"

CHAPTER FOUR
The Kitchen

On Saturday, June 8, 1996, we had our first strategy meeting: myself, Sarah Morton, and Liz—who had by now recovered sufficiently from her initial shock and horror to talk about the situation objectively.

Michael Rudge, one of the shining lights among the DA's four-hundred-and-some assistant district attorneys, had been assigned to cover the case, which was already notorious and destined to become a darling of the media. Rudge was a law-and-order man out of Harvard Law, and there was talk that he hoped to become the next DA. With him would be another assistant DA, Helen Slater, who, according to my records, had taken classes with me some nine years ago. I hardly remembered her. Mike Rudge, thoroughly and desperately a conviction DA, was about fifty, which is old for an assistant DA.

My agreement to be Liz's lawyer was nothing I would have suggested on my own. I succumbed to her pleading and tears after trying to explain to her the vast difference between a professor of contract law and a criminal lawyer. I had never tried a criminal case, and I would have been the last one to take the responsibility of defending Liz. Once I had agreed and accepted the fact that she would trust no one else, I turned to Sarah Morton. Her immediate response was to say, "You are absolutely crazy, Ike. I'm a people's defender. I've never had a high-profile case like this. I defend drug pushers and small-time crooks and muggers."

"I've watched you. You're the best damn criminal lawyer in the business."

It took some argument to persuade her, but after the grand jury had indicted Liz, she appeared with me at the bail hearing. In typical fashion, Rudge asked for half a million in bail; and here I was grateful for my many years of teaching. Alan Krisky, the judge, was Columbia Law and had taken classes with me. He said to Rudge, "The right to reasonable bail, Mr. Rudge, depends on character. She lives with Professor Goldman. The bail is twenty thousand dollars, cash or bond." It was a sort of inside joke, which Rudge did not appreciate, but I thanked God for the fact that Liz would not have to spend another night in jail.

I must say that if I had cared for her before, she was now my whole world. I had confessed to myself that I was wholly in love with this woman who had appeared one cold night on a bridge, intent upon killing herself. I use that endlessly misused word, *love,* a word utterly degraded in Hollywood dramas and films. This was no youthful crush or simple physical attraction. I had been living with some part of my soul absent, and no knowledge of what was missing and no real desire for it. Charlie had let drop once that he thought I was the father she had never known, but he was way off the mark. If there was any parenting, it came from her constant solicitude and understanding. Given that most love affairs between an older man and a much younger woman are incomprehensible to so many, I must perhaps leave this as such.

Tonight, when we sat down at my kitchen table for our first strategy meeting, she was more alive and alert than I had ever seen her to be. Her large gray eyes sparkled, her lips were set, and her lovely, small face was tuned to excitement. She had been through a great deal, an arrest for murder, a grand jury, a night in jail, and the sudden transformation from a totally unknown woman from Boston to an object of media fixation. If I had been asked a month ago what such a sequence of events would do to her, I would have thought that it would crush her. As she had said to me, "I'm not happy that he's dead. I never wanted anyone dead—much less a man for whom I once had feelings. But I'm released, Ike. Whatever happens now, I'm released, I'm free, and I love you; and it's like being born again. I'm ashamed of what I feel, but I welcome it."

"Nothing to be ashamed of," I had said. "It's a feeling many women have shared."

It had not been easy to persuade Sarah to come into the case. I talked her into accepting a ten-thousand-dollar retainer. I had investments in the market, my savings, and my pension. I was not poor, and I was not being fraternal in my desire to have Sarah on the case. On and off through my retirement years, I had sat in on criminal trials, and it had not resulted in great admiration for criminal lawyers. I admired Sarah.

Tonight, I laid out the situation as it was at the moment: "Liz, Sarah is as familiar with the facts as I am, but I want you totally in on this before we start our discussion. I respect you, and I respect your intelligence. Forensics has determined that Hopper was shot between eleven and twelve midnight. Since the air-conditioning is maintained through the weekend, they can't pin it any closer. On Friday night, the building closes at seven. That's when the lobby guard and the checkout man on the desk leave. Since the lock on the front door can be opened from the inside and then automatically locks after someone leaves, people who so desire can work past seven and let themselves out. But the history of the building is that few take advantage of this. On the four other weekday nights, the building closes an hour later.

"At midnight, the cleanup crew enters the building. They have keys and masters for the offices. The two lobby attendants also have keys. The men in the cleanup crew arrive together in one vehicle. Friday, they arrived at ten minutes after midnight."

"All together and accounted for?" Sarah asked.

"Absolutely."

"Do any of them have criminal records?"

"One of them—drug dealing when he was a kid, ten years ago. The cops checked them all out. The cops talked to all of them the night of the murder. For the moment, according to forensics, we can leave them out on a time measure."

"Who did the forensics?" Sarah wanted to know.

"Manhattan South, state of the art. Without going deeper into the cleaning crew at this moment, we come up with two possibilities. The first is that the killer is employed in the building. He or she—"

"Ike, why 'he or she'?" Sarah asked. "You don't buy the woman angle?"

"I buy it and I don't. We'll get to that. But man or woman, he or she would wait. Hopper would be working late or he might have arranged a meeting after closing hours at his office. Thereby the killer lets himself out. The second possibility is that Hopper arranged the meeting and let the killer in himself. As for an exit, in both cases it could be before or after the cleaning crew arrived. The cleaning crew couldn't come up with any details about the movements of the elevators. They move the elevators as they require them.

"The long and short of it is that someone carrying my gun ordered Hopper to write a check to Cash and stood behind him with the gun at his skull, and before he could sign the check, shot him dead. No useful fingerprints anywhere, or else too many of them. The detectives came up with nothing useful. Then, using a lipstick, the killer—presumably—wrote these words on a sheet of fax paper that he or she ripped out of Hopper's fax machine, 'Sweet journey, Billy,' and left the gun on the fax paper.

"Those are the facts as we have them. Forensics says that the lipstick is the same brand and shade that Liz uses—and maybe a million other women. So there, Liz, you have the situation that led to your arrest. The Boston cops filled in some of the details concerning Hopper's treatment of you. Now, Sarah, on the gun?"

I watched Sarah as she listened to all this. She was a very black woman, with a face like cut stone. She had never taken her eyes off my face—never glanced at Liz, just listened to me, her brow furrowing at times.

"Guns travel," she said. "On the street, a good

small gun is like money. It buys cash, or crack, or women, or anything else you need. But the first question, Ike, among ourselves, is this: Did you kill Hopper? I ask that with the understanding that I am both your legal counsel, if you should be so accused, as well as Liz's."

"No," I said.

"I ask the same question of her."

"Not likely," Liz said.

"You showed me where you kept the gun, Ike. How long since you opened that drawer?"

"Years. At least three. Before Lena died."

"It was there then?" Sarah asked.

"Yes."

"And since then, how many people, not your guests, have entered this apartment with you not present?"

"I can't come up with that, Sarah. Painters, paperhangers, rug cleaners, delivery boys, the super, the doorman, electricians, TV repairmen, a plumbing crew for three days—I could go on and on."

She turned to Elizabeth. "The way I hear it, Liz, you had two identical lipsticks, one in your bag and one in the bedroom. The obvious question, if you are the accused killer, is why you didn't get rid of them?"

"I was accused." Liz shrugged. "It wouldn't make much sense to keep them, would it?"

"No," Sarah said, "but Rudge is a sneaky guy and

he's going to turn somersaults for a conviction. He'll say you held onto the lipsticks for the same reason you gave me, as part of your innocent plea."

"That would be something, wouldn't it?" Liz said. "But Ike will tell you I'm not that clever."

"Put it another way," I said. "Innocence does not denote stupidity."

"Ike," Sarah said slowly, "I've watched you and this woman for weeks. A man's lady wronged—that's passionate stuff. It was your gun, your hate—that son of a bitch did it to the woman you love. Why didn't you kill him? Why didn't the cops arrest you?"

I looked at her for a long moment. "The lipstick?"

"Not enough."

"Ike would never ask for money," Liz said. "It would degrade him."

"The check was not signed."

"Ike couldn't even ask, and you should watch him when he has to kill a cockroach."

"I know Ike, too. But my gut feeling is that this is a woman's thing, not a man's. I know a cop at the first precinct, Annabelle Schwartz. Sharp woman. I'll bet she went in with the detectives. I'll talk to her. I imagine it was her gut feeling and that she convinced the detectives."

"Why is it a woman's thing?" I demanded. "Murder isn't a woman's thing, Sarah."

"Isn't it? How many battered wives have you defended, Ike?"

"Why didn't I kill Hopper? I had motive. My friends know how much I value Elizabeth. I know what he did to her. The cops questioned most of the people I know well, so they know how much I care for Liz—foolish old man, caught up by this young woman, my gun—"

"What are you two doing!" Liz cried. "Ike didn't kill anyone. I didn't kill anyone."

"Liz, Liz," Sarah said gently. "We're working it out. Murder one is not a game or a TV show. This is only the beginning. We have to work through every angle of this. The point is that Ike had every motive you had. He hated Hopper. He owned the gun. You didn't even know that he owned a gun, unless you went poking through the drawers in his bedroom."

"Maybe I did. How would the cops know?"

"That's it exactly," Sarah said. "That's what we're doing. What do the cops know that we don't know? Do you have any gloves?"

"Three pair. The detectives took them."

"What kind?"

"Two pair of kid, one of wool."

"That's by the book. Kid gloves are meaningless. But you see what we must do?"

"Yes, I'm beginning to understand," Liz admitted.

"And your alibis are worthless."

"Why? We were both here when it happened, in bed and asleep."

"The same bed?"

I looked at Liz, who nodded. "That night, Ike was very tired. He went to bed at nine. I wasn't tired, and I couldn't think of sleeping."

"Why?" Sarah asked. "I mean, why couldn't you sleep? What did you do?"

"Oh, Sarah, I was flying. Ike had just asked me to marry him, and we set the date. I love Ike very much, but he was always arguing that he was too old to get married again and always talking about how his silly libido had shrunk. You can't imagine how much of that I had to endure from this sweet, good man. But Friday he agreed. I told him to go to bed and that I had to walk and breathe some good fresh air, and I went out for a walk—" She paused as Sarah's face suddenly changed.

"You went out for a walk?" Sarah asked.

"Yes. Is that so terrible?"

"Maybe not. How long were you out?"

"Half an hour, forty minutes, possibly even an hour—I don't know. I walked up to Broadway and down to 103rd Street, and then back. My feet never touched the ground. All I could think of was that Ike wanted to marry me."

"And Gregory, the night man, he saw you come and go?"

Liz hesitated, then said, "No."

"Why not?"

"I went down on the service elevator and out on the side street. I do that sometimes. I took a piece of paper with me and folded it to keep the service door open until I got back. Everyone does it."

"Why didn't you go out the front entrance?" Sarah demanded.

"When I do and it's dark, Greg gives me a lecture on how dangerous the Drive is at night. It isn't, but he's a nervous Nellie. I was in no mood to discuss it with him. Did I do something wrong? My goodness, you don't think—"

"No, I don't think." She turned to me. "Ike, what time did Liz get back?"

"I don't know. I dozed off. All I remember is her cold feet when she crawled into bed. I kissed her. I didn't look at the clock."

"Oh, for God's sake, Sarah, you don't think I went down to Wall Street?"

"I don't think so, but what I think doesn't matter. Did anyone see you, coming or going?"

"No one that I know—no." Liz's confidence had vanished.

"I think I took a sleeping pill that night," I said. "I'm not sure."

"What kind of a pill?"

"A mild one. Temazepam, twenty milligrams."

"You don't and won't remember!" Sarah said sharply. And then to Liz, "Did you wear gloves when you went out?"

"Yes. Kid gloves."

"Did you wear gloves when you took the paper for the door?"

Liz, her brow furrowed, thought about it, then nodded. "Yes, the paper was an afterthought."

"Thank God," Sarah said, sighing. "If they find the paper, your prints won't be on it."

"I know what you're thinking," I told Sarah. "What do we do?"

"Nothing. Liz never left your bed. What did you do with the folded paper?" she asked Liz.

"I threw it away."

"What kind of paper did you use, Liz?"

"Just ordinary computer paper."

"Where did you throw it?"

"In the big garbage can."

"By now, they have it, if they know what it means. To hell with it. You never left Ike's bed, Liz. We never mention this to anyone—anyone—do you understand me? Liz could no more have gotten down to Wall Street that night and shot Hopper and gotten back in bed with you—no! No more than I could."

Liz was in tears now.

Rising, I walked around the table and kissed her. "We're going to beat this, baby. I promise you. Criminal trials are part evidence, part illusion, and part theater. I hate to be cynical, but the theater part is the most important. Sarah, I think, will agree with me, but when I see someone like you accused of a cold-blooded murder—well, I've known the district attorney for years, and I have a date to see him in his office next week. I'll ask him to drop the whole thing."

"I have a terrible headache," Liz whispered.

"Then lie down. Sarah and I can go on with this, and we'll be going over this again and again in the next few weeks. I'll get you some aspirin."

"And the wedding, Ike?"

"We'll get this trial over with, and then we'll be married." I took her into her room, embraced her, and said, "Come to my bed. I don't want you to sleep alone tonight."

"I will, Ike. I'll lie in the dark for a while and get rid of this headache, but I'll be in your bed."

I kissed her and went back to the kitchen. Sarah was speaking on the telephone, and as I entered, I heard her say, "As soon as you're free, Jerry, but within the week. Right?"

She put down the phone. "That was a man by the name of Jerry Brown, Ike. He's a private investigator but very smooth, very good-looking, and well dressed. The fact that he's black doesn't hurt; they bend over backward these days down on Wall Street for a smooth black man with no attitude. He's properly licensed, and he figures two or three days will do the job. He'll give us the names of any women at Garson, Weeds and Anderson who have been involved in any way with Hopper—and probably a good bit more. He's expensive, eight hundred a day, but we need him; and if you can't handle it, I'll pay it out of my retainer."

"I can handle it, no problem. But don't you think the cops have canvassed them?"

"Maybe," she said. "Or maybe not. The problem is the gun. As I told you, a stolen gun travels, and life is filled with coincidences; but still the gun is a mountain. How do we get across it?"

I shook my head hopelessly. "Coincidence. What else?"

"And the DA will not drop it. An election's coming, and this is meat and drink for the media. He wouldn't have put Rudge on it if he didn't want a conviction."

"We belong to the same club," I argued. "Every time he has an important contract crime, he lunches with me and talks about it. I never charged his office a dollar. He'll listen to me."

"We'll see," Sarah said. "Meanwhile, now that Liz is gone, we must talk about her." She lowered her voice. "You love her, Ike?"

"More than I ever dreamed I could love a woman."

"Do you know her?"

"Does a man ever know a woman?"

"Doesn't answer."

"She's a good, sweet, gentle woman. She's a believing Catholic. She goes to Mass and Communion every Sunday."

"Do you know me, Ike? I sing in the church choir. I'm a good Baptist. You were my teacher. I come here two nights a week and cook you dinner. I defend men I know are guilty. A woman can know a man, but no man really knows a woman. You've known her for a few months—how well?"

"Sarah, for God's sake, you don't think—" It was a whisper left unsaid.

"No, I don't think she killed him, but I don't know. The cops think she did and Rudge thinks she did. And we have to save her. That's my job. And she will have to take the stand."

"No!"

"Ike, she must. It's the only way."

"No—no, not with the man you tell me Rudge is. No, it's bad law."

"Ike, you're a dear man, but what do you know of criminal law? I have defended three women—two black and one white, battered wives who killed their husbands. And I put every one of them on the stand— the white one against Rudge—and I won. Why the hell are you hiring me if you won't listen to me?"

"I'm ready to listen, but to put that child on the stand?"

"She's no child. She's forty-eight next month. Ike, you can fire me and get some big media-type lawyer; but if you use me, you must listen to me."

"I listen to you, but I can't forget that I'm a lawyer."

"You're a teacher, not a litigator. You're an upright, decent human being whose stomach would crawl at the things some litigators do. I was born to be a litigator. So if you want me in this and you want to keep your love out of jail, listen to me. We have one witness that matters—Liz—and I pledge you that after I'm finished with her, Rudge won't do one damn thing to hurt her. Agreed?"

"Agreed."

"Now, I'm going to need a paralegal. I know a good one. She'll cost us thirty dollars an hour."

"Fine. What else?"

"I'll call you as a witness."

"OK."

"We have to rehearse it."

"OK. I'm totally available," I said. "But you have to keep me off the witness list, and then convince the judge."

"I'll take care of that. Now, is there any other way to get in and out of this building without being seen?"

"You're still harping on Liz."

"No. I don't believe she did it. Rudge does."

I sighed and shook my head. "No other way."

"What does that mean?" Sarah asked me.

"Never mind. Out—yes. The super lives in a basement apartment. The door there has one of those bar things; push the bar down and you can open the door. No key or keyhole. Deliveries from outside must press the buzzer."

"The back elevator runs all night? Could a perp press the down button and get out before the door closes?"

"I suppose so."

"I came up the back way tonight," Sarah said, "buzzed the buzzer and the door was opened by the super. I anticipated the back way might matter, and I thought I'd try it."

"So why ask me?"

"You live here. I don't, and I never came up the back way before. This is 1996. Could you fold a piece of paper and keep the back door from locking?"

"I suppose."

"Don't get nettled by me, Ike. It's my way. We have to work together. I was afraid of this when you talked me into taking this case. Now I'm not a student or a cook—I am a damn good criminal lawyer. I've defended pushers and pimps and killers and hookers, and, once, a woman who killed her two children."

Smiling wanly, I said, "I'm sorry, Sarah," feeling like a small boy being verbally whipped by his mother. "Did you get her off?"

"I did. She and the kids hadn't eaten for four days—too proud or crazy to beg, and too ignorant and too new to Harlem to know what else to do. The paralegal's name is Jane Johnson—we call her J. J. Now, it's going to be difficult if not impossible to work out of here. Can you make some arrangements for downtown?"

"I already have. Dave Friedman has a suite in the Woolworth Building, with a small room he can lend us. They use it as an extra storage place for the library, and it has tables and chairs. He does contract work exclusively, and he's happy as a clam to be able to watch a criminal case at close quarters. He was one of my students, and he's a decent young man. He assured me that we can use his copying machine and fax, but we'll have to rent a computer and printer. I'll take care of that. Can your J. J. take dictation?"

"She spent a year as a court reporter."

"Good. And about my attitude—you're the first counsel. You litigate. That's settled," I assured her. "But my world has changed, Sarah. I was living my death. Now, I'm living my life. This woman has given me life and hope, and she wants to have a child with me."

"Ike, she's—what—forty-seven, forty-eight? Besides, I thought she was barren."

"She is willing to adopt."

"Go slowly, please," Sarah begged me. "I've watched the two of you together. She's good and loving and innocent, but we have a mountain to climb. I wish this was uptown. I know one cop in the first precinct, and in Manhattan South I'm an uppity nigger. That doesn't bother me too much, but it would help if I weren't a stranger there. With Rudge, it's another matter; he hates my guts, and that helps. I want the jury to see him as someone who can't wait for a hanging. He has a good case, and he convinced the grand jury to indict without much trouble; but the grand jury's one thing and the trial is something else."

"You don't hold out much hope for my meeting with the District Attorney?"

"No. The very fact that he's an old friend mitigates against it. They have too much evidence and too much motive. If Jerry Brown finds motive in a few other women, it might help; but I want you to understand one thing, Ike: as matters stand now, at this moment, they have enough evidence for a conviction."

"All circumstantial."

"Ike, for God's sake, stop being a law professor and start to think like a criminal lawyer. If I had a dollar for every perp convicted on circumstantial evidence, I'd be rich. The woman you love, the woman you agreed to marry, faces the possibility of spending the rest of her life in prison. This is a carefully premeditated murder. The woman—"

"You keep saying 'woman,'" I interrupted. "You can't be sure of that. No one can be sure of that. Why can't we argue that a man is an equal possibility and my motive is as good as Liz's. Better, because I don't share her belief in God's justice or that vengeance is His. Why shouldn't I have killed him?"

"And used the lipstick? And implicated the woman you love? And sent her to prison? It won't wash. Anyway, Liz was their decision, and the lipstick makes me agree that a woman killed him. As I said, it was carefully premeditated. The woman made an appointment to see Hopper. She put the gun to the back of his head and ordered him to write a check for cash in the amount of one hundred thousand dollars. Cash, because a name on the check would have given the whole game away, and when he lifted his pen to sign it, she shot him. There's a beautiful gesture of hate—one hundred thousand dollars worth of hate."

"Liz didn't kill him."

"No, and that's what we're going to prove. We've talked enough tonight. I'm going home. I'll see you tomorrow, and we'll look at that space in the Woolworth Building."

Sarah left, and I turned off the lights and went into my bedroom. Liz had closed the door and was huddled under the covers and I thought she was asleep. I undressed quietly, but when I crawled into bed, she opened her eyes and kissed me.

"How is the headache?"

"All right now. The truth is, Ike, I couldn't talk

about it anymore, and I didn't want to hear you and Sarah talk about it, so I closed the door. Hold me in your arms, Ike, please—I'm so frightened."

I took her in my arms, her head on my shoulder.

"Ike, so many times I thought of him dead, of being released from my fear of him—in my heart, I wanted him dead. I have to face that."

"No, you don't have to face it and you don't have to think anymore about it."

"I love you, Ike."

"I know you do."

"You don't have to marry me, Ike. If you didn't want to marry me after all this, I'd understand."

"I want to marry you—more than I ever wanted anything."

"And you don't think I'm a murderer?"

"I don't think nonsense, and you're talking non-sense."

She fell asleep in my arms, but sleep did not come so easily for me. Suspicion is an ugly little monster that crawls through your brain and leaves dirty bits of doubt behind. Was it conceivable that Elizabeth had murdered this man who had abused her so? To me, it was not, and I can say truthfully that it had never entered my mind except as a seed planted there by others. Did Sarah believe that Liz was guilty? I know that the question of guilt or innocence is not the determining factor in the acceptance of a case by a criminal lawyer—then, what did Sarah believe? Why was she so insistent on putting Liz on the stand and thereby giving the unspeakable Rudge an opportunity to cross-examine? I knew Sarah, or at least a part of her, recalling her statement that no man really knows a woman. But she had come to my house twice a week after Lena's death—cooking for me and berating me for not eating enough to keep me alive—and again and again, we had talked for hours. I had gone to court at least a dozen times to watch her defend some wretched person, and I had watched her win cases that I felt could not be won, but to put Liz on the stand? What on earth did she have in mind?

Finally I fell asleep with Liz's warm body still cradled in my arms, her soft, easy breathing marking the sleep of innocence.

CHAPTER FIVE

The District Attorney

The district attorney rose from behind his mahogany desk to greet me and to shake hands. Should I take that as a bad sign or a good sign? I wondered. He could be sealing the bond of friendship, or he could be saying, "Nothing we say now, Ike, dissolves the fact that we are old friends." Nothing? He had already branded the woman I loved as a murderer, and he had assigned his most ferocious combat hound to bring her down.

"Ages since I've seen you. You look good—not a day older."

It wasn't "ages" by any means. A year ago we had sat for two hours at the Harvard Club, while I unraveled one of the most complicated contracts I had ever seen. Any other lawyer would have charged his office at least a thousand dollars for the work. To me, it was simply a favor for an old friend, paid for by the accolade that I was the best contract lawyer in New York. "Why you don't take up a practice, I don't know," he had said. "You're not that much older than I am. My word, there are a dozen firms that would roll out the red carpet for you." I told him that I like to read, that there were at least a hundred books I should have read and never had the time for.

"What can I do for you, Ike?" he asked me, as if he didn't know why I was there, and I refrained from saying that such pleasantries were beneath him at this moment.

Instead, I put an end to good fellowship by saying flatly, "You can drop the case against Elizabeth Hopper."

He regarded me for a long moment, and then said quietly, "You're angry, Ike. That doesn't help a serious discussion. Sit down. If you have your pipe with you, you can smoke—which is a favor I grant very few. Anyway, I love the scent of your tobacco."

I ignored that and sat in one of the carved chairs that faced his desk. Like many people from very good families, he had inherited good furniture as well as good taste.

"You want me 'to drop the case,'" he repeated.

"What? As a favor? You know I don't operate that way. You, above all people, should know that criminal law is based on evidence; and we did not thoughtlessly indict Mrs. Hopper. We have evidence, and the Grand Jury accepted our evidence. I had no alternative."

"And with over four hundred assistant DAs, you chose Michael Rudge to prosecute."

"He's senior, and he's good. He asked for it."

I calmed myself, knowing that anger would get me nowhere, and I said, "Every bit of evidence is circumstantial. You haven't one fact that places her at the scene of the crime. You will have my testimony that she was at my apartment in my bed at the time of the crime."

That had been decided by Sarah and myself. The truth of the matter was that when I awoke during the night of the murder, Liz was in bed with me, cold and clinging to me. The fact that I took a sleeping pill would not come up at all, and if it did, I would lie about it. The District Attorney made a point of that.

"Ike, you should know as well as I that a man and a woman in love with each other are worthless as witnesses. An old widower who has been married for years and who has experienced the agony of living alone and then finds a younger woman who loves him will lie under oath as easily as a hardened criminal. That's a given, but we won't call either of you as a witness. You say this case is circumstantial, but we have a motive that's overwhelming. We have sent an ADA to Boston, and the police are cooperating."

"And you still have no evidence that isn't circumstantial. Why not indict me? I had equal motive."

"We've discussed that, and we think otherwise."

"In other words, you intend to go ahead?"

"Unless you want to talk about a deal."

"No, thank you," I said bluntly, and got up and walked out of his office. Not very diplomatic; but if I lost a friend, I could tell myself that with such friends, one did not need enemies.

I was becoming increasingly disturbed as the trial date neared. The image of cold hatred that the murder evoked came into my mind again and again, and again and again I returned to the conviction that Liz was not capable of such hatred. I knew her too well, her gentleness, her innocence, her deep belief in God and God's justice. We had never argued about religion, indeed we had hardly discussed it seriously. Myself, I was an agnostic; whatever would be would be, and I was not too interested in delving into what could not be known. Yet, it was clear to me that my total belief and trust in Liz were not too widely shared. My friends at the university either offered condolences or avoided the subject. The media devoted itself to Hopper's scam with the fifteen million he had allegedly stolen and to the battered-wife thing, contrasting these with the two Olympic gold medals; and I consoled myself with the heroic vision of confessing to the murder myself if Liz were found guilty.

It was a warm, pleasant day; from the District Attorney's office, I walked to the Woolworth Building. I have always enjoyed the old skyscraper with its faded grace reminding me of a time long past, where hindsight made things rosier and better. Jerry Brown, the investigator Sarah had hired, arrived at the same time and shared the elevator with me. He was a tall, slender brown-skinned man, dressed with careful propriety—blue blazer, white shirt, gray flannels, and a bow tie. He was very handsome, and the women in the elevator could not keep their eyes off him. I greeted him warmly. He was very personable.

The office, so kindly lent to us by Dave Friedman, was about ten by fifteen feet, already crowded with a desk and office machines, and now, five people: Sarah and J. J., almost buried in a pile of books and transcripts; Liz, sitting in a chair and looking exhausted; and Brown and me. Liz, I learned, had been at it with Sarah for the past two hours, working over her testimony. There were no chairs for Brown and myself; and rejecting the offer of the women, we sat on the edge of the desk. Brown had finished his third day of investigation, and he reported from his notes in a small notebook. There was no air-conditioning in the room. I managed to open one of the windows, and we shed our jackets.

"I think I've done as much as can be done," Brown said. "At least I've widened the turf. There are twenty-two women working on the premises of Garson, Weeds and Anderson. Only one is in an executive position, and she's in her late fifties. Three are black, credit equal opportunity. That leaves eighteen. The black ladies caught my eye, but I don't think Hopper would have been interested, and none of these four use Autumn by Devlon. Of the eighteen, twelve are brunettes, and none of them use Autumn. Leaves six. Two of the six use no lipstick—in their forties and nothing to write home about—that leaves four possibilities, and three of them do use Autumn. Very nice, well-stacked ladies, all four of them. Names—take these down, J. J.—Lucy Dell, Nancy Carter, Josie Levine, Roselyn Craft. The last one doesn't use Autumn, and Nancy Carter lost hers. Left it in the ladies' room and it disappeared. Two of them, Nancy Carter and Roselyn Craft, admit to lunching with Hopper. None of them admit to a more intimate involvement. None of them express great dislike for Hopper, except that Lucy Dell—a very neat package—called Hopper a shit. Yes, used that word. Based it on what has floated back to her. None of the four worked directly for Hopper. The woman who acted as his secretary is a fluffy little blond in her forties and about thirty pounds overweight, and doesn't use Autumn. The cops checked out their alibis, but I can recheck if you want me to."

"How on earth did you get all this?" I wondered.

"The partners were very cooperative. They want this cleared up as soon as possible, and they turned the place over to me. There's one large con that Hopper was already involved in, and the murder on top of it does them no good at all."

"What about the partners?" Sarah asked him.

"I considered that, and I was very open about it. I'm not convinced that it was a woman, and I put that flatly to the partners. They showed me Hopper's account books and explained that his death made the recovery more difficult, since now there was no way of knowing which customers he had cheated and of how much. They said they desperately needed him alive. My experience with financial fraud is nil, but I can understand the advantage to them of having Hopper on the witness stand—and they can't have him now. I hate to say that being black gives you a foot in the door, but a tie and a three-piece suit helps. They're very conscious of political correctness, and anyway I don't see them in this caper. The cops established their alibis. There was a case in 1993 where a Wall Street player named Kessell hired a hit man who just happened to be a Fed. The financial crowd can be crooked as hell, but by and large they don't work it out with violence."

"Did you talk to the cops?" I asked him.

"I'm no great shakes downtown, and precinct number one is an odd kettle of fish. Aside from a couple of dark showpieces, they're as white as the driven snow. But they got a transfer from uptown, a neat piece of—well, she's something. A big, smart-ass gal, name of Annabelle Schwartz. I took her to lunch—dutch, she insisted—and she opened up some. It was like pulling teeth."

"You're good at pulling teeth," Sarah said. "I know Annabelle."

"I'm dry as a desert. You got a bottle of Coke some-where?"

"I'll get you one," J. J. said. She had listened to Brown adoringly, and she dived through the door to the main office and returned with an open bottle of cold Coke.

"I dry up when I talk," Brown explained, riffling the pages of his notebook. "We got along. She asked me if I ever dated a white woman. I told her it's absolutely politically correct in 1996, but she'd have to put the cop crap aside and let me take the tab. Then she went into the stupidity of detectives. She was the one who de-cided that it was a woman and talked the detectives into Manhattan South doing the match job. She also told me that the cops went through the cans of garbage—"

"You're taking notes, J. J.," Sarah said sharply. Then to Brown, "Where, Jerry? What cans of garbage?"

"In the basement of your building, Professor," Brown said to me. "I don't think they're as stupid as Annabelle does. They found a sheet of paper—Hewlett-Packard Multi Purpose, eight and a half by eleven—that was folded over and over until it made a wedge that could keep the outside door from locking itself. Trouble for them is it's not watermarked, and the same mill makes paper for other companies. I say Hewlett-Packard because that's the paper the professor uses, but as I said, it could be any brand that buys from that mill."

"They have to show it at discovery," Sarah said.

"Maybe not. It's a lousy piece of evidence. We could accuse them of folding it themselves, and they may just put it aside. There are no fingerprints—no fingerprints anywhere in this case. You ask me, they got a little bag of circumstantial evidence and absolutely nothing else. Now that adds up to what I got. I'm beginning another case, but anytime you want me, I'll make time."

"We'll see," Sarah said. "But thank you. We're grateful."

"I'll write you a check," I told him.

"Not a hell of a lot to be grateful for," Brown said. "Do you want my opinion?"

"Of course," I said.

"This is a political show trial, 'Olympic athlete, gold medal winner foully murdered.' It puts their names in the media. They can't place this little lady in the building between nine and twelve, and without that, they got nothing."

Elizabeth broke into tears after he had left.

"I've done an awful thing, Ike. God will never forgive me. You had a calm, decent life, then you saved my life and I repaid you by shattering yours to pieces."

"That's nonsense," I said, "and you know it is. You made an empty life worthwhile." I took her in my arms and held her. "All over soon, and then we'll put it behind us forever."

"No, we'll never put it behind us, and I'm so frightened," she whispered. "I'll always be a woman accused of murder, even if I don't spend the rest of my life in prison."

THE DISCOVERY PROCEDURE was held before Judge Rena Nussbaum. I could only hope and pray that she might be the trial judge, but I knew that was unlikely. She was a round, motherly woman—a description she had earned with the raising of five children—and she was a good lawyer. She listened patiently and thoughtfully to my motion to drop the charges and throw the case out. Sarah had insisted that I do the plea, leaving unsaid the fact that I was Jewish and that Judge Nussbaum was also Jewish. Rudge was cold and determined. Judge Nussbaum had the motion to dismiss for a week, and while I had hoped, I was not surprised by her rejection of the motion. The trial would take place. She called me up to the bench and said that she would see me and Sarah and Rudge in chambers.

Apparently she was no stranger to Sarah. "You're very wise, Ike," she said to me. The first name was the result of a number of social occasions we had spent together. "You have one of the best defenders in town, and I wouldn't trade her for any of the big names. Let me say too that Mr. Rudge is very experienced and very skilled. You will not mind my saying that, Mr. Rudge." He nodded.

"Thank you, Your Honor," Sarah said.

She had both witness lists on the desk in front of her. "I see Elizabeth Hopper as a witness. I don't know what Sarah has planned, but I feel it is my constitutional duty to remind you that Elizabeth Hopper cannot be forced to take the stand. I'm sure you know that; nevertheless, I want the record to show it. It would be wholly improper for me to ask what you have in mind."

"We have given it a lot of thought," Sarah said, which was the truth only in the sense that Sarah knew what she was doing and that I, while giving it thought, was nervous as a hen and would have argued violently against it had I not agreed to place myself and Liz in Sarah's hands.

"You have two weeks to the trial date," Judge Nussbaum said.

Walking back to the Woolworth Building, holding Elizabeth's hand in mine, I asked Sarah where we went from here. She replied with the story of a musician lost on Broadway who asked a bystander the way to Carnegie Hall. The answer was, "Practice, practice, practice."

"I wanted to be an actress," Sarah said. "My mother talked me out of it. Twenty years ago, the best chance a black actress had was welfare; and Mom, who supported us with washing and housecleaning, said she'd beg on the streets before she took welfare. She was from South Carolina—a preacher's daughter, God rest her soul—but the point I'm making, Liz, is that a criminal trial is theater. As a public defender—and I suppose I'll be one again when this is over—I had a caseload big enough for three attorneys. I managed somehow and did the best I could. But this is the first time I've had weeks to mull over the problem and to lie in bed at night planning my strategy—and I think I know what I'm doing. Nussbaum is a good woman, and she warned us about putting you on the stand. I had offers from the District Attorney to join his staff, partly because I'm black. But I'd take in washing before I'd become a prosecutor."

That evening, Liz and I had dinner at Romer's. Sarah had subpoenaed a part of the lipstick message and had a lab test it against a number of the most popular lipsticks on the market. The bill for the testing came to almost three thousand dollars, and indeed they did find three brands that were practically identical to Autumn, so close that the lab would not verify the difference. The three lipsticks were sent to another lab, which also refused to confirm a difference, and that cost another eleven hundred dollars.

At dinner, Liz brought this up. She had barely tasted her food, and suddenly her eyes filled with tears. "Don't," I said to her. "Please, I can't stand to see you cry."

"I was thinking of those lab tests. Ike, this is costing you thousands and thousands of dollars. I have no right to impose this on you. I am pauperizing you, and I'm not worth it, Ike. From the beginning I've brought you nothing but grief. What must your family think of what I'm doing?"

"You're not pauperizing me, and if you'll wipe away those tears and eat your dinner, we'll talk about it. What my friends think, I really don't give a damn. If they're friends, they'll stay with me. Charlie Brown, my best friend, is so envious of me he'd change places in a minute. I have Social Security. I have a good pen-sion, and I have a lifelong stack of securities and bonds. What am I supposed to do with it? Even Rockefeller couldn't figure out any way to take it with him. This is the second time today you've wept—and that hurts, believe me. If you have a bit of concern for me, you won't do it again."

She smiled—the first time today. "Ike, does it re-ally hurt you when I cry?"

"It sure does."

"Then I won't cry again. At least I'll try not to, ever—except on the witness stand. Sarah said I could cry."

"That's OK."

"And maybe at our wedding—if you still want to marry me?"

"Absolutely. I can understand that."

"Even if they find me guilty?"

"Liz, Liz—they will not find you guilty."

"But your family, Ike. What does your son think of all this?"

"My son, Danny, as you know, Liz, is comfortably ensconced in Washington. He has a wife and three chil-dren—my family, finis. He works as operations man-ager for Bill Gates, and aside from perks and stock options, he earns two hundred and seventy-five thou-sand a year. When I telephoned him a few weeks ago and laid out the situation, he said, 'Go for it, Pop; and if you need money, let me know.' So much for your concern about my family. Now please eat your dinner."

Later, in bed with my arms around her, she whispered, "I feel safe, Ike. Here, with your arms around me, nothing in the world can touch me. Oh, I love you so; I just love you so much."

CHAPTER SIX

Charlie Brown

WHEN YOU REACH MY AGE, friends become fewer and increasingly precious. I can write down the names of a hundred people I know well enough to call and receive a pleasant reply when they pick up the telephone, but they're in another category. Take the District Attorney for example. On and off, I had known him for at least twenty-five years—but as a friend? When had I dined at his house? When had he reached out to me for other than a favor—*you, Ike, the best mind in New York on contracts*—when? To be used is flattering, and a man loves flattery. When I was young, I turned to older people. I suppose that's only natural for someone in my position, but you grow old and they pass away; and then you come to an age when each friend is a particular jewel, very valued. If you have, at my age, half a dozen of such, you are a fortunate man indeed.

Charlie Brown was an old, good friend. He called and said we must talk—and seriously—and I met him in the faculty lounge at the university a few days following my visit to the District Attorney. After some words about the weather, Mayor Giuliani, and the gonadal drive of our president, he turned to his profession and remarked that he liked to think of himself as a good shrink, if only because one learns more through teaching than practicing—although he had never given up his practice.

"The point is," he said, "that teaching, one never surrenders the process of self-examination. Teaching, you must examine and explain. The kids demand it. The patients don't."

"Which leads you where, Charlie?"

"To places where angels fear to tread. I want to talk to you as a psychologist and as a dear friend. You're a proud man, Ike, and as soon as I step out of line, you're going to be sore as hell at me. I want to avoid that."

I shrugged. "Let's see."

"You've never gone in for psychoanalysis, have you?"

"No. It's not my thing, Charlie."

"Well, it has its value, however besmirched the good Sigmund is these days."

"You don't think that Burns said it all when he wrote, 'Oh wad some power the giftie gie us, / To see ourselves as others see us'? The trouble is that the good Lord withholds that giftie very jealously. Of course, one makes guesses, Charlie. Here's old Ike with a woman half his age whom he had decided to be in love with. You're almost old enough to remember the Peaches Browning case. An old man loves a young woman, and he becomes a clown, and the tabloids have a great basket of plums. Add murder, and you even knock the terrorists off the front page. We're obsessed with murder, Charlie. It's the great American thing. What could you possibly say to me that would be any worse than what our great media has already done to me and to that poor woman whose soul has been torn to shreds by a monster?"

"Are you in love, Ike?"

I thought about that for a while before I answered. "Kids fall in love. It's a process of the ductless glands, a gift from a God who desired this thing we call the human race to perpetuate itself—for what purpose I surely don't know."

Charlie nodded and waited.

"I'm a lonely old man. Is that what you were going to tell me?"

"Partly."

"And I'm Jewish."

"Thank God, I'm not," Charlie said. "Too many guilts."

"I mean I saved her life. I owe her."

"No. She owes you."

"I see it differently, but we're not going to argue about that."

"No. I want to talk about this objectively. I've been following the case, reading every word about it I can find. You can't fault me for that."

"You and several million others."

"They're not your friends, Ike. I don't enjoy seeing you mauled and hurt. Fame is the curse of our society, and this kind of fame is absolutely the worst. I'm not here with apologies. I want to help you."

"Charlie, I don't need help."

"Oh, but you damn well do. Now I'm out of line, and if I go on talking, I'll be even more out of line. Either you listen to what I have to say, or you tell me to shut up and that's the end of it."

"No. I want to hear everything you have to say."

"Clint Gordon was here the other day. He lectured at the Law School, and afterwards, he was in here having a drink. Someone introduced him to me. Very curious about an old friend of Ike Goldman—I suppose because he's professionally pissed off at your hiring Sarah Morton instead of some big player like himself. Of course, he sees himself as king shit in criminal cases, and those bastards are all ego. He feels that the people have a solid case and that your Elizabeth will spend the rest of her life in prison."

"I'm not impressed."

"He wanted to know whether I knew Liz, and what did I think psychologically."

"What do you think psychologically?"

"Do you want to hear that from me?"

"Yes, I do."

"All right. The gesture of having Hopper write out a check for one hundred thousand dollars and then putting a bullet into his head before he could sign it signifies a hatred so filled with rage and contempt that it calls for a history. You told me that Elizabeth has a history of abuse and even what can be considered torture, both physical and mental. If her history of what she suffered at the hand of Hopper can be trusted—even the little you have told me—and if in all that time she never fought back, never resisted, then the rage has been bottled up."

I took out my pipe and stuffed it.

"They don't like that here," Charlie said.

"I won't light it. So you think Liz killed him?"

"Put yourself in her place."

"I can't do that, Charlie. No one can inhabit another's mind. I was married for years, and now when I look back, I realize how little I knew my wife. Men and women—there's an ocean between us. Men make wars and kill."

"Have you ever faced the thought that Liz might have killed him?"

"No. Liz could not kill a rabbit."

"Hopper was not a rabbit. Would you have killed him, if you'd had the opportunity?"

"Where is this leading us, Charlie?"

"You told me you had decided to marry her."

"Yes."

"You're standing by that?"

"Yes."

"Ike—Ike, my dear friend—for God's sake, think. Who is she? She's a stray you found on a bridge, with no background, no family, no education, and a Catholic—a Catholic, Ike."

By now, I was blazing inside, but I controlled myself. There's no cord attached to words spoken in rage; you can't pull them back. Charlie Brown was the best friend I had in this life, and I was too old to make new ones. "Charlie," I said softly, "what kind of a background do I come from?"

"Your father was a judge."

"Charlie, did I give you that impression? My pop was a Justice of the Peace. There were only seven Jewish families in Oneonta then. He had a tailor shop. They made him JP because they wanted a Jew on the town council—just to show how broad-minded they were. And what's this about Liz being a Catholic?"

"Sorry. I should not have said that, Ike. But it's a different world."

"Oh, is it? Charlie, just allow me a word or two about this waif. She's fluent in Latin. I've been trying to read Tacitus in the original. She translates on sight, as she reads. Her French is perfect, and she knows more about art than anyone I ever met. When we go to a museum, I ask the questions and she answers them. I've talked more deeply to her and more openly in a week than I did with Lena in a lifetime. She loves me, and for the first time in my life I have the feeling of being really cherished. I am the luckiest man on earth. Instead of dying bit by bit, I have her. Why she wants me, I don't know, though I did save her life. She was crushed almost to death by that bastard she was married to—and then, day by day, what was in her unfolded and freed itself. You think she could have killed Hopper. Charlie, she didn't kill him. I know that."

"You're thinking that it's hard to kill. You're a man of peace, and you can't face the very notion of taking another man's life."

By now, I was becoming tired of the whole discussion. What kind of gift was Charlie bringing me? Swallowing my anger, I told myself that I would not lose my temper, I would not hit back at him, I would not thank him for trying to convince me that I must not plan to marry a murderer. I took the words from him and said, "But you're convinced that she will not win, that she'll be found guilty and sentenced to life in prison?"

"That's what Clint Gordon said."

"And what would you advise, my friend?"

"Right now, you hate my guts," Charlie said.

"No, I don't."

"Then bring someone like Gordon into the case and wash your hands of it."

"Oh, Jesus, Charlie!" I sighed, almost at a loss for words. "You know, like so many Jews, I could fantasize myself with a gun to Adolf Hitler's head. I couldn't pull the trigger."

"I could. Oh, shit—why did I ever start this?"

"You care for me. Thank God, a few people do."

That was the end of my discussion with Charlie. We shook hands and remained friends, but he had cut deep. The easiest person to doubt is oneself. What did I know of Elizabeth Hopper? I had made myself a picture of her as a simple, direct, and open person, but had defended her to Charlie as a well-educated and complex woman who could read Tacitus in the original Latin, who knew more of art than I had ever dreamed of knowing. My wife, Lena, had been direct and open, content with being a teacher of mathematics and dedicated to her single child and to myself. I had known her entirely, or at least I thought so. I knew her family,

her friends, her dreams. If I didn't adore her passion-
ately, I had lived happily with her.

And I told Charlie, fervently, that Liz was incapable
of murder. But Charlie obviously didn't believe that,
and the District Attorney did not believe that. I knew
one thing about the Irish—they dissemble easily. The
thought that Liz would steal my gun, put me in harm's
way, and use it to kill a man whom she loathed, was
something I had never countenanced. But it faced me
now.

It was not that they had a shaky case against Liz—
and evidently Clint Gordon felt it was far from shaky—
it was the thought that she had taken my gun.

I dismissed it. I told myself that even the thought
was beyond decency, and I would never allow it into
my mind again. But the thought did not dismiss me.

CHAPTER SEVEN
The Trial

I HAD NOT ANTICIPATED the ravenous interest the trial would arouse in the media, but after all, it was the trial of a woman accused of murdering a notorious Wall Street broker and one-time Olympic star, already in the news for doing his clients out of fifteen million dollars. It had all the elements required to arouse a jaded public, tired of the O. J. Simpson trial and the arguments its aftermath had provoked, and the battered wife and the lipstick note brought everyone in, from the *New York Times* to the television networks.

Judge David Kilpatrick presided, an elderly gentleman with long sideburns and a large mustache, and small steely blue eyes that promised nothing for

anyone. I had never met him, which I now felt was all
to the good. When he walked in for the first time, he
made a simple statement: "I will tolerate no disorder in
my court—no disorder of any kind. I want that understood."

Sarah had given me a quick rundown on him:
"He's utterly technical and very good. A walking re-
pository of law. He's a sour man, but equally for the defense and the prosecution. A good Catholic. Married
over forty years to the same woman, two daughters.
But expect no sympathy from him on that count."

He was good in the selection of the jury. He came
down hard on Rudge's attempt to load the jury with
men, and we ended up with three black women and
two white women. The remaining seven were men,
but three alternates were women, one black. Sarah was
more than satisfied. Rudge had run out of preemptors
when we accepted a black woman named Fay Jones.
Sarah's mother had known her. She was a woman in
her fifties who had done housework and put her son
through college. Sarah had never met her, but Sarah's
mother had talked about her with endless admiration.
She had married a worthless bum who had beaten her
and then walked out on her forever when her son was
three years old. Three of the men were married. One
was a widower.

Rudge's assistant, Helen Slater, had been a student
of mine at Columbia Law. I remembered her now as a

bright, perky young woman, who even then was determined to become a prosecutor. She shook hands with
me decently and wished me the best, saying, "Who ever
thought, Professor, that I'd be working against you. I
know you can't wish me the best."

"I'm afraid I can't," I replied, rather surly. This was
neither a game nor a drama to me.

"It's how the cards fall," she said cheerily, and I
thought about what Sarah had said of a criminal trial as
theater. I was still somewhat uncertain about what
Sarah's trial plan was, although we had discussed it and
I had the gist of it watching her rehearse.

Liz was strangely calm. She told me that she had
gone to confession a few days before the trial began,
and she was at peace with herself. In the months that
had passed since I met her, I had thought that I knew
her, body and soul, better indeed than I had ever
known Lena, my wife; but this present Liz, a woman
facing life in prison, made me wonder. I had read somewhere that a Catholic who kills can confess to murder
and receive absolution if he or she professes repen-
tance, a determination never to repeat the offense, and
a belief in God. As I have said, I disliked myself for even
harboring the thought of this, and my own belief in a
just God was far from firm. But the woman who sat be-
side me in the courtroom, her small hands folded in
her lap, her face calm and reposed, made me realize
that there were depths in her I never plumbed. Here

she was on trial for murder, with the possibility of spending the rest of her life in prison; then where was the hopeless, terrified woman I had seen on the bridge? Had I done this? Then, whatever she might have done was also a part of my doing. Yet, still I attempted to believe in her totally, and I told myself again and again that she was innocent.

Rudge's opening statement was rather flat and straightforward and shorter than I had expected; but Sarah told me that opening statements were soon forgotten in what followed, and that Rudge very consciously built his case from a slow beginning. He began by saying that the state intended to prove that a cold, callous, and premeditated murder had been committed by the defendant, Mrs. Elizabeth Hopper. Then he laid out the details of the case according to the police reports. Then he said, "The defense will attempt to convince you that all of the evidence we intend to present is entirely circumstantial. What is circumstantial evidence? Unless the police have a reliable witness to a murder, then all evidence becomes circumstantial. The dictionary defines circumstantial as having to do with circumstances surrounding a fact. Every fact, every action, exists in what we might call a pool of circumstances. That is the nature of reality. We look at motive for a crime, and the facts of motive depend on a series of circumstances. No man or woman lives apart from reality, and what is reality but a set of circumstances? Were we not to depend on circumstantial evidence, few crimes would be solved. Now the state intends to call a series of witnesses who will testify to the facts and circumstances surrounding this vicious and premeditated killing. You, as the jury, will be responsible for putting together the pieces. If the pieces fit and make a perfect pattern, you will have no other choice than to find the defendant guilty."

When he finished, the judge said, "Would you approach."

Sarah and I, and Rudge and Slater walked up to the bench; and Judge Kilpatrick said softly, "I did not interrupt you, Mr. Rudge, but I will have no prejudgment. You phrased it cleverly, but the jury does have a choice. You cannot make it for them. Remember that, all of you."

It was a very mild reprimand, but it pleased me; and when the court broke for lunch, before Sarah's opening statement, I told her what I felt.

"He's meticulous," Sarah said, "but don't let it fool you. He's not leaning one way or another."

Sarah's opening was made that afternoon. Like Rudge, she began with a detailed itemization of the police events, but it fascinated me to hear how different it sounded as Sarah put it forth. She was speaking about a crime that had been committed somewhere, on Wall Street in this case, by one of many people who had reason to wish William Sedgwick Hopper dead. She itemized the members of the firm—the three partners whose names headed the list and the junior partners, the dozens of men and women who worked for Garson, Weeds and Anderson, the cleaning crew, the concierge—and then concluded by saying, "I neither accuse nor attempt to implicate any of this list of almost a hundred men and women. That is not my function. My function is simply to defend a good and innocent and gentle woman who has been chosen out of this large group of people to stand trial here with her life as forfeit for a crime she did not commit.

"The District Attorney made a long statement about circumstantial evidence. His definition was quite correct, and each name I have given you here is part of the circumstances of this case. He was careful not to tell you that the police found not a single fingerprint that belonged to Mrs. Hopper. What did they find? They found a note written with lipstick, and that happened to be a lipstick used by literally hundreds of thousands of women, some of them working at the same firm. Their so-called circumstantial evidence is so shoddy that if I were a district attorney, I would be ashamed to produce it. I intend to prove the innocence of Elizabeth Hopper. I beg you to keep that in mind. At this point, I know that she is innocent.

"This court, according to our law, must presume that she is innocent; and Mr. Rudge intends to prove her guilt beyond reasonable doubt. I see no basis for their intention. I put this question to you, as twelve men and women who will hear all the evidence. I ask only that you listen and weigh the evidence fairly and thoughtfully, and this I know you will do. If you have doubts that are reasonable, you must find her innocent. Thank you for being here."

The court broke after Sarah finished her opening; and we went back to my apartment together, all of us, including J. J. Sarah had sent Jerry Brown to Boston, and he was due back this same evening and would meet us at the apartment. He arrived at about five o'clock, and we decided to send out for Chinese. But when Sarah opened the door for Brown, she said to him, "You bastard, you waited until the last minute! You should have had this stuff a week ago!"

"Honeychile, it'll be a week before the state finishes their case. You got plenty of time." He came into the living room and plopped his briefcase down on the coffee table and stared at Liz.

"We don't have plenty of time!" Sarah snapped. "And why are you looking at Liz like that?"

"Because she's as pretty as a doll, and according to Boston, she took more punishment than Muhammad Ali. Two hospitals and three police stations—and the Boston cops are not good on race, no sir. They see a black man and double the charge. I put out three hundred bucks for copies of the damn records. What a corrupt bunch of bastards!"

"You have all of it?"

"All I could get, xeroxed and notarized. Give me a break, Sarah."

"A break? We're paying you eight hundred a day and expenses, and you want a break?" She was rummaging through the papers in his briefcase.

"Liz's going to phone for Chinese," I told them. "Will you please tell me what you want?" I asked, feeling that the argument between Brown and Sarah had gone far enough.

"I love Chinese," Brown said. "My favorite is pork fried rice—or anything else. Ah, Sarah," he said to her, "be a doll and smile at me."

"This is very good stuff," she admitted. "Very good."

"Give me a kiss."

Liz was laughing. It was a long time since I had seen her laugh. She phoned out for a vast order of Chinese food, and finally we dragged Sarah away from the pile of documents that the briefcase contained. We stuffed ourselves with Chinese food, and I told Sarah that I thought her opening was damn good.

"What would you have said if I had done something like that in class?"

"An interesting question. Of course, it's no opening for a contract case, but it's still an interesting thought. It's hard for me to think of myself as a teacher in the middle of this case. I must say I miss teaching."

"Then why don't you teach again?" Liz demanded.

"I don't know. I'm old—"

"You're not old."

"Liz, I was never happy after Lena died. But I was sort of content. I actually read Proust's great boring novel, and I read *War and Peace* for a second time. Now I'm happy but not content."

"I told you, Ike," Sarah said, "we will win."

"She ain't just whistling 'Dixie,'" Brown put in. "Professor, you got the best damn defense lawyer in the business." He looked at her adoringly. "She has a mean temper and she's too good-looking for her own good—"

"Oh, shut up!" Sarah cried. "Flattery will get you nowhere, and for you to talk about being good-looking turns me off."

"Well, he is very good-looking," J. J. put in, rather timidly.

"And what about Annabelle?" Sarah demanded. "I told you two weeks ago to see Annabelle again and get me the whole story."

"I don't make passes at white women."

"That'll be the day. Your notion of virtue—"

Brown spread his hands. "I talked to Annabelle."

"I hope you talked sweet."

"Sweet as butter. The detectives and Joe Kennedy, her partner, didn't have a clue. You know she said it was a woman, her idea. The others argued with her, but she's a tough lady. She convinced them it was a woman—the way it was done. She said no man would do a killing that way because no man could develop the kind of frustrated hatred that was inherent in the nature of the crime."

"On the basis of the lipstick?"

"She says she felt it, woman's intuition."

"Good," Sarah admitted grudgingly. "I talked to her and got nothing. Now would you and J. J. go home? Ike and I have work to do with Liz."

"Tonight?" Liz protested.

"And every other night."

I gave up at ten o'clock, and it was not until an hour later that Sarah left and Liz crawled into bed next to me. I woke up, as she snuggled into my arms and kissed me. "I'm tired," I said. "I'm old and tired."

"You're not old and not too tired to kiss me."

I kissed her, and we lay there in silence for a while. Wide awake now, I asked her what all this bickering between Brown and Sarah was about.

"Don't you know?"

"There's a great deal that I don't know. I don't even know what was in that briefcase Brown brought back from Boston. My position in this is purely titular."

"It is not. Sarah consults you constantly."

"About what she intends to do," I said. "What's with her and Jerry Brown?"

"They lived together for five years. Then she threw him out. She says he's great at what he does, but when it comes to women, he's a no-good bum. Those are her words. I think he's darling, and J. J. is madly in love with him. I don't blame her."

"What does that mean—that you 'don't blame her'?"

She snuggled closer. "Oh, Ike, you're jealous."

"You think he's darling."

"Ike, I love you so much there are no words for it. I will never love anyone else. I never have. I never could. My life is yours, entirely and always."

She fell asleep after that, curled up against me, my arm under her head, and I couldn't bring myself to pull my arm out and awaken her. Unless she changed her position, my arm would be dead in the morning— well, for a few minutes at least.

I didn't sleep easily, thinking of what Charlie had once said about there being no fool like an old fool in love with a young woman—and yet he added that he'd change places with me in a moment. *Let me be an old fool,* I thought, *but don't take her away from me;* and then I wondered to whom I was addressing the thought? Would I end up like Liz, believing in what was still utterly unbelievable—that someone or something or some force looked after me, and that nothing happened that was not ordained to happen? It was not a comforting thought; I preferred a system that was malleable and subject to change.

Neither was another thought: the *given* in a nation of law that when one is a prisoner in the dock, confronting whichever district attorney faces and prosecutes you, then you are likely enough guilty, in spite of the legend that no man or woman is guilty until proven so, beyond a reasonable doubt. As a lifelong professor of law, I should know and uphold the law; but what one knows intellectually does not always stand up against a lifetime of immersion in the media. A man builds a bridge, and he knows that every calculation has been correct—every measurement, every bit of steel and concrete—and then the bridge collapses.

Murder is the deepest, darkest stain against the human race that exists; it is also the deepest, darkest mystery—which is why it holds an endless fascination for us. You open a newspaper and stare at the picture of two small boys' round, innocent, beautiful faces—the faces of choir boys, loving children—then you read on to discover that these same two children have murdered their mother and father . . . and there is no reason or explanation ever to tell us why, and the mystery remains unsolved.

These are thoughts. My arm is around a woman who has brought a dried-up old weed to life. Was it a wise man or a fool who said that he who saves a human life saves the whole world? And what of he or she who takes a human life?

Liz, next to me, slept the sleep of the innocent, and I prayed to a God I hardly believed in that some of that innocence would seep into whatever soul I had.

CHAPTER EIGHT
The People's Case

THE PEOPLE BEGAN its case by calling Alec Prosky as its first witness. "Rudge is methodical," Sarah whispered to me. "He will pile on facts and more facts even when he has no facts, counting on the accumulation of detail to impress the jury."

Prosky stated his name and took the oath.

"What is your work?" Rudge asked. "Would you describe it, Mr. Prosky?"

"I work for Kelvin Kleaners. We clean office buildings after the people who work there have left."

"We, I take it, means you are part of a crew."

"Yes, sir." Prosky, a burly man in his thirties, was a mixture of awe and pride. Here he was, in the great

Greco-Roman-style building that housed the New York Supreme Court, as the first witness in a sensational murder case that had been headline news for weeks.

"How many men are in the crew?"

"It depends on the building. For the Omnibus, we use six. Frank Goober is the job boss." Prosky was gaining assurance as he spoke.

"What time do you begin at the Omnibus Building?"

"Midnight."

"And where were you at twelve-thirty A.M. on May twenty-fifth, 1996?"

"I was working the seventeenth floor, the offices of Garson, Weeds and Anderson."

"Alone? No one was working the floor with you?"

"No, sir," Prosky said. "I was alone."

"Please tell us what happened at twelve-thirty of that night."

"I opened the door of Mr. Hopper's office, and I seen him sitting at his desk. Sometimes some of the people there work late, and at first I thought he might be asleep. He was bent over the desk. I decided to wake him before I began to vacuum, and then when I went over to his desk, I seen the bullet hole in the back of his head and blood on his neck and the collar of his shirt, so I know he's dead."

"Did you touch anything there in the office?"

"No, sir. I didn't even plug in the vacuum."

"And what did you do then?"

"I took the elevator down to the lobby. Frank Goober was at the desk, filling in his charge book. I told him what I had seen, and he called 911, and then he said I should go up and see that nobody entered the office until the cops—I mean police—came, and he'd stay downstairs and let them in."

"Did you go into the room, into Mr. Hopper's office, again?"

"No, sir. I stood by the door until the cops came."

Goober, the next witness, merely confirmed what Prosky said. When the police came, Goober opened the front door for them. He took them up to the seventeenth floor in one of the elevators, and then he and Prosky were told to go back to the lobby and wait for the detectives.

Sitting next to me, Liz reached for my hand under the table. With her small, warm hand in mine, all my doubts vanished and I was suffused with a need to protect her. Aside from me, she had no one in the whole world to turn to. Her father had abandoned her mother and disappeared years ago. Her mother had raised her, and her mother was dead. She had some vague knowledge of an aunt in Los Angeles, whom she had never seen or communicated with; and she knew that her father had two brothers, but who they were and where they were, she didn't know. At first it had appeared impossible to me that a human being could

be so alone, so unconnected. Though we had been together for months now, I asked myself how well did I
know this woman? That she loved me, I had no doubt,
and on my part, old man that I was, I cherished and
adored her. Circumstances had placed her in my care,
and I had already worked out in my mind a complicated confession of my own guilt if she should be
found guilty. I was quite sure that I could prove to the
satisfaction of a court that I had killed William Sedgwick Hopper out of rage for what he had done. If I had
to spend what few years I might have left in prison, I
would at least have the comfort of knowing that Liz's
young life was not wasted. I now recognize how fool-
ishly romantic this notion was—and I had spoken
about it to no one—but it served to ease my days in
the courthouse.

The next witness the State called was Officer Annabelle Schwartz. She was something—six feet tall,
blond, and good-looking in her neat blue police uniform. She took the oath, nodded at the jury, and
smiled slightly at Rudge. Sarah had waived any cross-
examination of the first two witnesses, but I knew she
would lock horns with Annabelle.

"Officer Schwartz," Rudge said, "where were you
on May twenty-fifth between twelve and two A.M.?"

"On patrol with my rabbi, Officer Kennedy."

"Would you explain to the jury what you mean by
your 'rabbi'?"

"Oh, this is absolutely no disrespect for Jews or rabbis. It's a term the police use for an old hand who takes a freshman cop under his wing and teaches him the ins and outs of policing. When I was transferred to the first precinct, they assigned me to patrol with Officer Joe Kennedy, who is smart and experienced. We were on Broadway when the call came from the precinct, and we drove immediately to the Omnibus Building."

"At what time, Officer?"

"Twelve-fifty."

"Please tell the jury what happened then."

"We parked. Goober opened the building door for us, and we went up to the seventeenth floor. Goober led us to Mr. Hopper's office, and then we told him to go down to the lobby and let in the detectives and the morgue wagon and the forensics people. Prosky opened the door, and we went into Mr. Hopper's office. We did not touch or move anything. A few minutes later, Detective Sergeant Hull and Detective Flannery arrived and began their examination of the crime scene. Mr. Hopper was dead at his desk, with a bullet hole in the back of his head. There was a long sheet of paper on the desk, torn from the fax machine, and on it, in red lipstick, words were printed in block letters. It said SWEET JOURNEY, BILLY. A Colt twenty-two caliber automatic pistol was sitting on the sheet of paper."

"Is this the sheet of fax paper you refer to, Officer Schwartz?"

"Yes, except that a piece of it is missing."

"The State offers this as evidence," Rudge said to the judge, "with the explanation that the missing piece was given to the defense for their laboratory work."

"So marked and entered," the clerk said.

"Do you have anything else to add?" Rudge asked Annabelle.

She hesitated, and then said, "Yes, I offered the opinion that the murderer was a woman."

"And what brought you to this notion, Officer?"

"A number of things. The lipstick, the intimacy of the killer and Hopper, the revenge implication—very feminine, I think—the nature of the message on the fax paper."

"Thank you," Rudge said, and turned to Sarah.

"Will you cross-examine?" the judge asked.

"If you please, Your Honor." Sarah stood almost as tall as Annabelle, and said to her, "So you knew immediately that the perpetrator was a woman—is that not so, Officer Schwartz?"

"Well—yes. I felt it."

"And why did you feel it?"

Again, Annabelle hesitated. "I guess because of the reasons I just gave." Again she hesitated. "And the small gun, which would fit easily into a woman's purse."

"Oh. Remarkable. Did the detectives have the same

immediate reaction? Did they say it was a woman perpetrator?"

"No," Annabelle admitted. "But when I explained to them about the lipstick, they sort of agreed."

"Sort of. What does sort of mean?"

"Well, when I told them what the lipstick was—when they asked me whether I knew—they tended to agree."

"And what lipstick was it?"

"Devlon Autumn."

"How remarkable," Sarah said, turning to the jury. "Now, I do not use Autumn—partly because I have black hair. Now I suppose"—turning back to Annabelle—"that if I asked my boyfriend to buy me Autumn, they wouldn't sell it to him. Do you agree, Officer Schwartz?"

For a long moment, Annabelle was confused. She shook her head. "Why shouldn't they sell it to him?"

"I'm asking the questions, Officer. Would they or would they not sell it to him? Yes or no?"

Rudge half rose to object, but Judge Kilpatrick waved him back, saying softly, "The door is wide open, Mr. Rudge."

"Yes, they would sell it to him," Annabelle admitted.

"Or to any other man who said the price?"

"Yes."

"How many Autumn lipsticks did the Devlon Company sell in 1995?"

"I don't know."

"You don't? I'm surprised. Why don't you know?"

"Because I'm not a detective," Annabelle replied with some indignation. "I'm a uniformed police officer, and I don't follow up on a case. That's the work of the detectives."

"But I should have thought that Mr. Rudge, who argues here for the State, would have told you. My investigator, Jerry Brown, went to the Devlon Company and they were only too pleased to tell him."

"Save your remarks," Judge Kilpatrick said. "If you want to get into that, frame it as a question, Ms. Morton."

"Yes, your honor. Now, Officer Schwartz, would it surprise you to know that the Devlon Company sold 3,090,000 sticks of Autumn in 1995?"

Annabelle shrugged.

"Please answer the question," the judge said.

"No, it would not surprise me!" Annabelle snapped.

"And since you've already admitted that a man could buy a stick of Autumn, how do you come to the conclusion that a woman wrote those words on the fax paper?"

"It wasn't only the lipstick."

"Ah—then there was other evidence? What was the other evidence, Officer Schwartz?"

Sarah had said that criminal trial is theater. There are probably thousands of decent, upright people with the name of Schwartz, but in every film and TV show about the Nazis, there is some evil character with the name of Schwartz—due, perhaps, to the lack of imagination among Hollywood writers. Now Sarah's constant repetition of the name and the magnificent blond largeness of Annabelle was reflecting on the jury's perception of the witness.

Annabelle replied, "The use of the name *Billy,* for one thing. It's a name a woman would use for a man she had been intimate with."

"Oh, I see. And does that mean that a man who calls his friend Billy or his son Billy is—what should we say—a homosexual, a transvestite? Or what?"

"You're trying to confuse me!" Annabelle cried.

"Not at all," Sarah said smiling. "Please answer the question."

"What was the question?"

"Would you read it?" Sarah asked the stenographer.

The stenographer read it, and Annabelle said, "No, it has nothing to do with homosexuals."

"Thank goodness," Sarah said. "They have enough problems." The judge glanced at her, and she asked quickly, "Is that the sum of your decision that the murder was committed by a woman?"

"I mentioned the small gun."

"So you did," Sarah agreed. "But, Officer Schwartz, as a police officer, you carry a gun, don't you?"

"Yes. Of course I do."

"And when you're not in uniform, where do you carry it?"

"In my purse."

"Ah, so your gun is small enough to fit into your purse?"

"I have a large purse, and my gun is not a twenty-two."

"And would it surprise you to hear that at least three hundred murders in New York City last year were committed with twenty-two caliber guns, and most of them by men?"

"I don't know the figures, but it wouldn't surprise me," Annabelle said. She had recovered her composure.

"Have we exhausted all the deeply impressive and valid bits of evidence that brought you to the firm conclusion that the death of William Sedgwick Hopper was caused by a woman, or is there more? Fingerprints, for example?"

"There were no fingerprints—"

"How would you know?" Sarah interrupted

sharply. "Are you intimate with the detectives, Officer Schwartz?"

"I talked about the case. I *do* work in the same precinct."

"But the fingerprint work was done by Manhattan South. You don't work there. Surely there were hundreds of fingerprints in Hopper's office? Were there not?"

"I'm not familiar with the fingerprint matching. I hear there were none that implicated anyone."

"Wonderful!"

"I'm a woman," Annabelle snapped. "I have the right to see things as a woman."

"So you are, so you are. I would not deny that for a moment, Officer Schwartz. Did you perhaps smell an odor of perfume?"

"No!" she snapped.

"Or a trace of face powder on the gun?"

"No!" Then she added, "I have the intuition of a woman."

I knew this was what Sarah had been looking for, and I glanced at Rudge, who closed his eyes for a moment and compressed his lips.

Sarah was facing the jury. "A woman's intuition," she repeated. "Well, why not? I suppose I relied on my intuition when I was briefly married, but I also looked at the clock when he came home with no explanation—"

"Ms. Morton," Kilpatrick said sternly, "no more of that. Save it."

"I'm sorry, Your Honor." And to Annabelle, "Are you also psychic, Officer Schwartz?"

"No, I am not psychic."

"I have no more questions for this witness," Sarah said.

"Any redirect, Mr. Rudge?" Judge Kilpatrick asked.

"None, Your Honor."

"Then we'll break for lunch. The court will reconvene at half past one." At lunch, I said to Sarah, "That was awfully good. Why didn't Rudge prepare her more carefully?"

"How could he?" Liz wondered. "He couldn't have known what Sarah would ask."

"He didn't anticipate that she would blurt out her woman's intuition," Sarah said. "That's a wonderful peg for me to hang onto. I hate to do this to Annabelle. She wants desperately to be a good cop; I know her, and she's really a nice girl. And smart."

I felt more than ever that I had been right in talking Sarah into this. Bit by bit, I was coming to know her better—a strange, complex woman who assumed an air of confidence and mastery in court that as yet Rudge appeared unable to cope with. Possibly Rudge's reputation had been inflated, but more likely the problem of facing a black woman defending a white woman had thrown him off his stride.

Especially since Sarah had already done so success-fully.

And Liz was changing as well. The change in Liz had been slow in coming; from the beaten, broken woman I had met on the bridge, a new personality was coming into being. The trial excited her, and she no longer wept at the possibility of fifteen years to life in prison. She had left her job of selling women's shoes two days after the arrest, although with her name making headlines in the *Post* and the *Daily News,* she could hardly have kept it, in any case. She had spent most of the time since then with Sarah, whom she had come almost to worship. When I first met her, she had been hollow cheeked and lean, almost anorexic. She had filled out now, not fat, but becoming increasingly lovely. She had cut her mop of blonde hair quite short, and she looked ten years younger than forty-seven. Never in all my life had I been the recipient of such gentle love and comfort. She seemed to anticipate my every wish. If I left my pipe in another room, it appeared in her hand before I could ask for it. If I felt any of the arthritic pain that comes with age, she knew it before I spoke and soothed me. The media was dying to interview her and write the story of her bitter marriage to Hopper, but Sarah forbade it absolutely. No one of us spoke to the media, so Rudge had the spotlight. There was talk that he had expectations of being a top

District Attorney, if not for Manhattan then perhaps for Brooklyn.

Hopper's misdeeds at the investment bank moved from the *Wall Street Journal* and the *New York Times* financial section to the tabloids and the media; and since some of my friends at Columbia had loose tongues—to put the best face on it—they also went into the romance between a seventy-eight-year-old and a forty-seven-year-old. Fortunately, my friends were decent enough not to mention the incident on the bridge.

When we finished lunch and made our way back to the court, Rudge put Detective Hull on the stand. He covered all of what Annabelle had testified to, and then Rudge began to weave his net: "Did you have the lipstick on the fax paper analyzed, Detective Hull?"

"Yes, sir. I brought it to the forensics department at Manhattan South. They confirmed that it was Autumn."

"I have here their report," Rudge said, handing a sheet of paper to Hull. "Do you recognize it?"

"Yes, this is it."

Rudge entered it as evidence, and then he asked Hull, "What was your next step in this investigation, Detective Hull?"

"The pistol, which as I said was lying on the sheet of fax paper. I picked it up, using a pencil, and gave it a cursory examination. I saw no fingerprints. Neither did the fingerprint man from Manhattan South, who arrived while we were still in the office. He wrapped the pistol in a plastic bag and took that and the fax paper to the forensics department at Manhattan South. Since this was late night—or early morning, to be exact—he said that they would study the fingerprints in the office the following day. Mr. Hopper's body was taken to pathology for autopsy."

"Did you check the registration on the pistol?"

"Not that night. But the following day, Manhattan South reported that the pistol was registered to Professor Isaac Goldman, and that it had been purchased by him on the ninth of December in the year 1977. They also analyzed the lipstick on the fax paper and reported that it was Autumn, manufactured by Devlon. We ascertained that Mrs. Elizabeth Hopper, the divorced wife of William Sedgwick Hopper, had been residing at the same address as Professor Goldman, to whom the gun was registered. We—and when I say 'we,' I include my partner in the investigation, Detective Joseph Flannery—well, we decided that at this point in time, we had sufficient evidence to obtain a search warrant, which we obtained from Judge Lyman Ferguson, at the Superior Court. We then went to the residence of Professor Goldman and made our search."

He then went on to relate the details of the search and the arrest of Liz.

"After the arrest of Mrs. Hopper, did you question

the other women who worked at the offices of Garson, Weeds and Anderson?"

"We questioned all of them."

"How many women were involved in your investigation? I mean, how many women worked for Garson, Weeds and Anderson?"

"Twenty-two."

"And did you question all of them?"

"Yes, we did. We discovered that only four of them had any more than the most casual contact with the deceased. We felt that all of them had proof of their movements that night."

"Did you check out these proofs, as you call them?"

"We did, and we concluded that it would have been impossible for any of them to have been in the Omnibus Building that night at ten o'clock, which forensics had placed as the time of Mr. Hopper's death."

"How did you determine that Mrs. Hopper was able to be at the Omnibus Building at ten o'clock on the evening of May twenty-fourth?"

Hull was proud of the methods of the New York Police Department. He told the jury how he and his partner, Detective Flannery, had timed the trip to Wall Street and back and then had canvassed my neighborhood drugstores to find out which one I patronized and had gotten my prescription for Temazepam.

"I have been assured," Hull said, "that in a tablet of twenty milligrams, Temazepam promotes sound sleep.

Such was the conclusion of Dr. Vinelli at the Manhattan South testing lab."

Judge Kilpatrick looked at Sarah for an objection, but she shrugged. "I'm sure it does," Sarah said.

"And what did you conclude from this?" Rudge asked.

Now Sarah objected, but mildly. "I am sure Mr. Rudge knows better than to ask a question that calls for a conclusion by asking in advance for a conclusion."

Muted laughter from around the court and from Liz as well, who whispered to me, "She's ragging him, Ike. He's so angry!"

Liz was right. Rudge was a dominating, aggressive prosecutor, and Sarah was puncturing his ego. This kind of defender was new to him.

"Phrase your question another way," the judge said.

"What did you do next?" Rudge asked, changing direction.

"Detective Flannery and me, we emptied the rubbish can that was just inside the back door. There we found a piece of paper, which was folded back and forth until it was large enough to prevent the back door from closing. It had dirt on the outside fold which matched the dirt on the door sill. This was the result of laboratory tests."

Rudge then offered the folded piece of paper as testimony, and it was passed around for the jury to see.

"Is the paper exactly as you found it?" from Rudge.

"Oh, yes. We were exceptionally careful with it. You will notice the sharpness of the fold in the center of the final fold. That's where the door and the paper came together."

Hull went on to expound on his theory: When I was sound asleep, Liz had slipped out of the apartment and had taken the elevator down to the basement. According to Hull, she had then fixed the basement door to reopen, using the folded sheet of paper he had presented as evidence. She had previously arranged with Hopper to meet her at the door to the Omnibus Building and thus admit her. She had used my gun, readily available to her, to kill Hopper, after forcing him to write the check. She had acted out of hatred and her need for revenge.

It did not come out exactly that way. Twice, Judge Kilpatrick called us up to the bench, disturbed by Sarah's unwillingness to object to this testimony; and three times he took upon himself the task of ordering the court recorder to expunge it.

"Needless to say, I am disturbed by your attitude," he told Sarah. And to Rudge, "Certainly, you know better than to have a witness make your closing argument. I am willing to give you leeway, Mr. Rudge, but this is too much. You will confine your questions to what Detective Hull has knowledge of, not his speculations."

Rudge stated his right to recall Detective Hull, and then Kilpatrick asked whether Sarah had cross-examination.

"Oh, but I do, Your Honor," Sarah said. She rose, walked across to the jury box, nodded at the jurors, and then, turning halfway, asked Hull, "When you first entered the crime scene and looked at all the elements, you expressed the feeling that a man had killed Mr. Hopper. Did you not?"

"Well—" he hesitated. "I wouldn't say that."

"What would you say, Detective?"

"One naturally thinks of the murderer as a man."

"Oh, one does? Then how is it that I have defended so many battered women who killed their husbands?"

"I suppose it's different in Harlem. This is Wall Street."

"According to the testimony of Officer Schwartz, she decided it was a woman, exercising, as she put it, her woman's intuition. Is that not so?"

"Yes."

"So the murderer became a woman?"

"We felt that she had made a reasonable guess," Hull said.

"You do a great deal of guessing, Detective Hull, do you not?"

"We try not to guess. We go after evidence."

"How did you determine that the gun that killed Mr. Hopper was the same gun you found on the desk?"

"We sent the gun to Manhattan South. The bullet was taken from the corpse. Manhattan South matched them."

"I see. Detective, you have heard the phrase 'guns travel' used by the police. Would you please tell the jury what that phrase means?"

Hull glanced at Rudge, who nodded, and then Hull said, "It means that after a perpetrator uses a gun, he sells it to someone else or dumps it."

"Now, how many murders were committed in 1995 with a twenty-two caliber pistol?"

Rudge objected, but Kilpatrick said he would allow it if Sarah connected it. Hull answered that he did not know the figure.

"Ten, twenty, a hundred?"

"I don't know."

"If I told you that it was well over three hundred, would that sound reasonable?"

"I suppose so."

"And did you ask forensics at Manhattan South or the FBI to try a match between the bullets from these many other murders with the bullet that killed Mr. Hopper?"

"I saw no reason to. We had the gun and the bullet, and we traced the gun to the suspect."

"But as you testified, the gun belonged to Professor Goldman, who stated that it was stolen. He is not the suspect, is he?"

"No, he is not."

"And you testified that he stated that the gun might well have been stolen months or years before. Is that not so?"

"Yes."

"So, isn't it possible that for the past several years, this same gun might have killed another person before it came into the possession of the murderer—"

Rudge rose to object, but the judge said that it was a reasonable question and that he would allow it.

"I don't know," Hull replied.

"You should know, Detective. It's your business to know. Now, is it or is it not a reasonable presumption?"

I began to feel that Hull did not know what to make of Sarah. Here was this tall black woman using him, and evidently he did not enjoy being used. He was losing his calm and certainty.

"Answer the question," the judge said.

"I suppose so," Hull admitted.

"And if this crime had taken place in the 33rd or 34th precinct, or in the 79th, for example,"—Sarah turned to the jury—"high homicide precincts, all of them"—and back to Hull—"if this had been the case, they would have sent a complex of the bullet to both the FBI and to forensics for matching, would they not?"

"I work in the first precinct."

"What does your answer mean? Does it mean that if a complex of the bullet had been sent out for matching, this trial might not have taken place?"

Before Hull could answer, Rudge rose to object, and the judge agreed that Sarah was stretching it too far. "Keep to the facts, Ms. Morton."

"There are no facts," Sarah said gently.

"That's quite enough, Ms. Morton. Don't push it."

"I'm sorry, Your Honor."

She walked back to the table and riffled through her pile of papers. The judge asked her whether she had finished her cross-examination.

"Not quite, Your Honor," turning back to Hull. "Tell me, Detective, did you consult a pharmacologist as to the exact nature and effect of Temazepam, taken in doses of twenty milligrams?"

"We discussed it with the pharmacist who filled the prescription for Professor Goldman."

"And what did he tell you?"

Rudge objected, arguing that the defense could call the pharmacist as a witness, if they so desired.

"Ms. Morton?" the judge asked.

"It goes to the credibility of Detective Hull's investigation, Your Honor."

"I'll allow it," the judge agreed.

"Well, Detective?"

"He said it was a sleeping pill."

"Did he say what sort of sleeping pill?"

"At this level, a mild one."

"Detective Hull, did you ask Professor Goldman whether he had taken a sleeping pill that Friday night?"

"No, but his prescription read whenever he had difficulty sleeping."

"More intuition," Sarah said, smiling slightly. "But here is my question. Mr. Hopper was killed Friday night. Five days later, with only four intervening days, you arrested Elizabeth Hopper. You testified that twenty-two women worked at the offices of Garson, Weed and Anderson. Now I have great admiration for the New York City plainclothes force, but is it possible that you tracked down these twenty-two women, just you and Detective Flannery, in these four days, considering that two were weekend days, Saturday and Sunday?"

Hull hesitated for a long moment before he said, "No, we didn't speak to all of them in the four days."

"Ah, then perhaps Manhattan South assigned a special task force to help you?"

"No. Detective Flannery and I did the interviewing."

"All twenty-two?"

"Well—" Hull hesitated, and then put his foot into

Sarah's trap. "No, not all twenty-two. He had a girl-friend in Boston, and we spoke to the Boston Police. She had an ironclad alibi. We didn't speak to her then."

"And the twenty-two women at Garson, Weeds and Anderson?"

"Like I said, not all twenty-two."

"Why not all twenty-two?"

"Well, you know, before the arrest of Mrs. Hopper, we questioned the most likely ones."

"And how did you decide which were most likely?"

"But eventually we questioned all of them."

"You haven't answered my question," Sarah said sharply.

"Well, you know, women who he, I mean Hopper, would have been attracted to. He had a reputation of being a womanizer. We put off questioning the older women, and there were three Afro-American women—"

"Who could not have been attractive enough to interest Mr. Hopper," Sarah said sarcastically. "Is that what you were going to say?"

Hull shook his head without answering.

"I have no other questions for this witness," Sarah said, her voice tinged with contempt.

Rudge's next witness was Abel Johnson, the super-intendent at my Riverside Drive building. He was a large, good-natured black man. He took the witness stand and the oath, then grinned at me and Liz.

"Mr. Johnson," Rudge said, "would you tell the jury where you work?"

"I'm the superintendent at the building where Professor Goldman lives."

"And how long have you been superintendent at this building?"

"Eighteen years. It's a good job."

"And I'm sure you do it well. Now, do you watch television?"

"I sure do. I'm not much of a newspaper reader. I usually watch the six o'clock news on ABC and the ten o'clock news on Channel 11."

"Were you watching the news on Saturday, May twenty-fifth?"

"I sure was. I remember the day because Greg— he's the night man in front—he got this little radio of his on all night. Keeps him awake, you know; and he tell me in the morning that Mr. Hopper got shot, and we know Miss Liz's name is Hopper."

"So you made the connection. Otherwise you might have forgotten that precise date? Is that not so?"

"I suppose. But I watched TV the same day, you know."

"Now, tell me, Mr. Johnson, do you recall anything unusual happening on Friday night, the night before, say between ten and midnight?"

"Midnight, I'm asleep. I don't have no trouble sleeping."

"But before you went to bed?"

Johnson had the jury now. He was enjoying his moment in the sun, and I'm sure he had no idea whether he was helping or hurting Liz's case. Witnesses do not sit in court before they are called, so he had not heard the openings or the other witnesses.

"Like what?"

"Like the basement door opening or closing?"

"No, sir, I wouldn't hear that, and you know, I'm watching the television. Then Missus and me, we go to bed."

"But the back elevator, you would hear that?" Rudge insisted.

"Yup. We're on the bottom floor. The back elevator, it go up quietlike but down with a bang. You see, nothing but cement and the bumpers. We look out on the air shaft, and it's pretty quiet."

"But you do hear the elevator hit bottom—with a bang, as you say?"

"Yes, sir. We look out on the air shaft, so there ain't much noise. But we do hear that elevator when it hit bottom."

"And did you hear it that Friday night?"

"I guess I hear it most every night. Late deliveries— or maybe some tenant, he want to leave by the side entrance."

"But that night? Can you remember?"

"No, sir—maybe yes, maybe no."

Rudge went to his table and opened a folder, and then turned back to Johnson. "But when the police questioned you, you stated that you had heard the bump that night—at least twice?"

"Did I say that? A long time ago—"

"That's what you said, is it not?"

"The cops say so, I said it."

"Thank you. The courtyard is lit all night, isn't it?"

"Yes sir. We keep it lit."

"Did you happen to look out of your window and see anyone pass by?"

Abel Johnson hesitated, just for a moment, and then said, "No, sir."

"When the police questioned you, you said you thought you saw a shadow move?"

"Maybe so, but I don't remember. We have curtains."

"And you can't identify the person as more than a shadow?"

"No, sir."

"No more questions for this witness," Rudge said with annoyance.

"Will you cross-examine, Ms. Morton?"

"Please, Your Honor." She rose and walked to the jury rail and said to Johnson, "The elevator bumps every night, Mr. Johnson?"

"Sure does."

"Who comes and goes so late?"

"Could be someone, he don't want Greg to see him. Or like maybe he parked on the side street and don't want to walk around the corner at night. Or maybe someone want a delivery, maybe like booze or something, so he don't want to wake me up so late and he go down to the basement and make sure the door is open."

"Does he? And how does he do that?"

Rudge rose with an objection that the question called for a conclusion; but Kilpatrick, a twinkle in his eye, said, "You've opened so many doors, Mr. Rudge, that I don't think your objection is valid. So let the witness answer the question."

"They all use the same trick," Johnson said. "Fold up a piece of paper and stick part of it under the door. Keep the door from locking. I see it all the time, you know. The insurance people raise hell, and the head of the tenant committee, you know, he promise a new door but never get around to it. New steel door got to be maybe eight hundred dollars."

"Thank you," Sarah said, walking back to the table and taking up some papers in a blue binder. "I'm through with this witness, Your Honor. May I approach?"

The judge nodded, and as Sarah walked toward the bench, Rudge rose to join her. Helen Slater, Rudge's assistant and coprosecutor, had as yet spoken not a single word. But then, neither had I; and as she was going to the bench, I decided to join them.

"If this closes the State's case—and from his witness list, I presume that it does—I would like to make a motion for dismissal of all charges." She placed the blue folder on the judge's bench. "Basically, for lack of evidence."

"You have my objection," Rudge said.

"I'll see you all in chambers," Kilpatrick said. Then he tapped with his gavel and said, "This court stands in recess. We will resume tomorrow at ten o'clock."

I asked Liz to wait for us at the table and then joined the others in the judge's chambers. Kilpatrick, a tall, thin man with brooding blue eyes and glasses, looked at us gloomily before he spoke. "Sit down," he said, and then to Sarah, "I'll look at your motion tonight and give you an answer in the morning. Off the cuff, I can say that I am in no way disposed to dismiss the charges, but we'll see. You're a damn clever lawyer, Ms. Morton, but I must say I am troubled by your listing Mrs. Hopper as a witness. I don't like people waiving their right against self-incrimination."

"I have given it a great deal of thought, Your Honor."

"I hope you're not reaching for a mistrial?"

"And go up against Mr. Rudge again? No, Your Honor, once is enough."

"Thank you, Sarah," Rudge said.

"But I do have one request, Your Honor," Sarah said meekly. She could become meek and gentle—this woman who had come up against all the odds.

"Yes?" Kilpatrick said warily.

"I would like to call my cocounsel, Professor Goldman, as a witness."

Rudge exploded. "Out of the blue! Your Honor, this is the first I heard of this! It's outrageous! The man listens to my evidence, my witnesses, and now he comes on the scene as a witness? I must object. This is without precedent."

"It's not without precedent, Mr. Rudge. For example in Callahan versus the State, in 1954, it was permitted, and I could cite you several more cases, if you like."

"Ms. Morton, when did you arrive at this decision?"

"Today, listening to the testimony of Detective Sergeant Hull. Put it to my own stupidity. I am taking the risk of putting Mrs. Hopper on the stand, but the point of the sleeping pills was made so forcefully that I felt I must have Professor Goldman on the stand."

I'm afraid this was by no means true. We had discussed my testimony. But this was Sarah's case, and I had agreed to play it her way. Not in a thousand years would I claim that I could creep into the soul and mind of another person, but here was Sarah with her first big case—a case that would change her entire future career. At this moment, I remembered her sitting in my classroom and listening to my opening remarks, when I told my students that contract law was all law, that every human relationship was a contract of sorts, whether with a client or the state or the codified law of centuries of human experience.

"You understand, Ms. Morton, that if I accede to your request, I must take Professor Goldman away from your table?"

"I understand that, Your Honor."

"And of course you do, Professor Goldman?"

"Yes."

"He will be my first witness, and I give you my word that I will not recall him."

"I enter my objection, most formally," Rudge said. He had control of himself now.

"Mr. Rudge, I am going to overrule you. This will give you an opportunity to cross-examine Professor Goldman. Since he is integral to this case, I am surprised that you did not call him as a witness yourself. This is a capital case, and a woman's life is at stake."

"Exception!" Rudge declared.

"Yes, I will take note of that," said Kilpatrick, clearly annoyed.

"Your Honor," Sarah said, "since the woman in this case is pledged to marry Professor Goldman, and since I have given my word that I will not recall him—I beg you that he be allowed to remain in the courtroom. In a way, his own life is at stake."

Kilpatrick studied Sarah thoughtfully. A slight smile crossed his face. "You were Professor Goldman's student, weren't you?"

"Yes. Contract law at Columbia."

"Back in '72 or '74—were you the first Afro-American student at Columbia?"

"No, not the first. But one of very few—I think the first woman."

"I see no reason why he should not sit in the courtroom, but not at the table; and you are not to speak to him or consult him at any time in my court."

"Thank you, Your Honor," Sarah said humbly.

When it came to playing Kilpatrick, Rudge did not hold a candle to her.

When we left the courtroom, with Liz and J. J., Sarah's feet never quite touched the ground. We went to Romer's for dinner, and Sarah ordered a steak and baked potato and finished it—to the last bite. Liz nibbled away at a salad. I had little appetite, but J. J. packed away a good dinner; and the only time Sarah mentioned the events of the day was to say that Kilpatrick was a pussycat—the last description of him that I would have thought of—and that there'd be no talk of the case tonight. "We've talked enough, Ike," she said. "I want to see a movie."

J. J., a soft and rather pretty woman, pleaded a date, so the three of us wandered on upper Broadway until we found a theater playing *Total Recall,* with Arnold Schwarzenegger. "I love him," Sarah said surprisingly. "He's all muscle and just enough brains to make fifty million a year—a perfect symbol of manhood."

Whatever the actor's shortcomings, we enjoyed the film and came out of the theater two hours later, feeling pleased and renewed. "Because it made no sense at all," Liz decided. "It's the perfect counterpart of the life we're living today. This trial makes no sense either. I could be guilty or innocent, but there's no way to prove either one."

"What I really liked," Sarah offered, "is that the black guy is a bad guy. I'm so sick of pictures that lie to make us feel good, with black guys as presidential advisors and saving the world from aliens and being hotshot detectives who know all the answers, when I've defended more black bums than I can remember, and some good guys, too. You're absolutely right, Liz, the life we're in doesn't make a shred of sense."

"Ike dozed off," Liz said. "Darling Ike, I've seen you sit through concerts without ever dozing. How could you fall asleep?"

"Because I'm old and tired, Liz. So, let's go home to bed."

CHAPTER NINE

The Defense

WHEN THE COURT CONVENED the following morning, Judge Kilpatrick asked that Rudge and Sarah approach the bench. I had seated myself in the first row, behind Liz, who turned to give me a warm smile. There was a buzz in the press section about my change of position, but that change would be explained when Sarah called me as her first witness. As I learned later, Judge Kilpatrick had told Sarah he was denying her motion to drop the charges, admitting that, so far, the case was entirely based on circumstantial evidence but positing that the evidence was strong enough to put the case to the jury. Then the court came to order, and I was called as Sarah's first witness.

I took my place on the witness stand, identified myself, and was sworn in. Sarah's first question caught me by surprise. "Professor Goldman," she said, "you were supposed to have married Elizabeth Hopper a few months ago. Is that not so?"

"Yes. We postponed the wedding until after this trial."

"I ask this question for the benefit of the jury. As a law professor, you are well aware that as her husband, you could not be forced to give any testimony against her."

"Yes, that is so."

"Yet, you did not marry her?"

"No. Not yet."

"Why, Professor?"

"Because I had hoped that the prosecution would call me as a witness, and I wanted no impediment to their doing so."

"And why, may I ask?"

"Because I know she is innocent," I said simply.

"Would you tell the ladies and gentlemen of the jury the basis for this belief on your part?"

"On the twenty-fourth of May, 1996, the night when the murder of William Sedgwick Hopper took place, Liz Hopper was in bed with me. She did not leave the bed until seven o'clock in the morning."

"Now, Mr. Rudge has elicited from a local drugstore the fact that you had filled a prescription for

Temazepam. Would you tell us something about this drug?"

Rudge objected on the grounds that I was not a pharmacist.

"But he has been using this medicine. I'll allow it," the judge said.

"At twenty milligrams, the amount in the pills I use, it's a mild sleeping drug. Occasionally, when I have trouble falling asleep, I take a single capsule. It has no aftereffects or side effects that I am aware of."

"And on the night of the murder, did you take Temazepam?"

"No, I did not," I replied, thinking that if I lied so easily on behalf of someone I loved, then what was the worth of an oath as the way to the truth? But I had no qualms about that while I was testifying. I believed wholly that Liz had nothing to do with the murder, so to me the lie was meaningless. I would have lied a thousand times to save her from a life behind bars.

"But did you go to bed earlier than the defendant?"

"Yes, about a half hour earlier."

"What time was that?" Sarah asked.

"Nine o'clock."

"And Mrs. Hopper joined you at nine-thirty. Were you awake?"

"Yes."

"Did she always share your bed? I understand that there is another bedroom in your apartment."

"When we first started our relationship, she occasionally slept in my son's room. I must explain that he lives in California. But after she moved into my apartment, she always slept with me in my bedroom."

"And when was that?"

"The first week of April—April third, I believe."

"Now, Professor Goldman, do you sleep soundly through the night without awakening?"

"No. As far as I know, no man of my age does—"

Rudge interrupted with an objection: "He is not a statistician or a physician."

"Mr. Rudge," the judge said, "he has qualified his statement by saying as far as he knows. I'm going to allow it. You may continue, Professor. The objection is overruled."

"I was going to say," I continued, "that from what I have read and from discussions with my contemporaries, most men over sixty-five—and I am seventy-eight—wake up to urinate once or twice, or even three times during the night. This, I am told, is due to an enlargement of the prostate gland with age; and my own pattern is closer to three times. Usually, I awaken an hour after I fall asleep. When I awakened to urinate an hour later, Elizabeth was sound asleep next to me."

"How do you know it was an hour later?"

"We have a clock in the bedroom. The face of the clock is lit."

"What time was it then?"

"Ten-thirty."

"How are you able to recall this so precisely?" Sarah asked.

"Five days later, the police appeared with a search warrant. That was when they arrested Elizabeth. When she was released on bail, we recalled the hours and noted them for reference."

"So according to your testimony it would have been impossible for Mrs. Hopper to have left your apartment, traveled to Wall Street, killed Mr. Hopper, and then returned to your bed?"

"Absolutely impossible."

Rudge had already objected: "Calls for a conclusion."

The judge agreed with Rudge and admonished the jury to ignore my statement.

"Is it inconceivable to you that Mrs. Hopper could have committed a murder—a deliberate murder such as this was described to the jury?"

Once again, Rudge objected that this called for a conclusion.

"I agree," Kilpatrick said. "Look up the word in your dictionary, Ms. Morton."

"Yes," I said. "Inconceivable."

"The jury will ignore that remark," the judge said crossly.

"I have no more questions for this witness," Sarah said.

Rudge stood up for the cross-examination, and said, "Do you love the defendant, Professor Goldman?"

"Yes."

"And you intend to marry her?"

I expected Sarah to object, but she did not.

"Yes," I replied.

"And would you lie to save her life?"

"That's outrageous!" Sarah cried. "I do object."

"Sustained," the judge said. "And you should know better, Mr. Rudge. The witness is under oath."

"I'm sorry, Your Honor," Rudge said. Sarah was getting under his skin. He didn't know how to deal with her, and the scathing attack he usually launched at criminal-defense lawyers was not applicable here. You don't humiliate and put down a black woman with the whole media alert. Also, there was no harmony between him and Judge Kilpatrick.

"Do you ever take more than a single twenty-milligram dose of Temazepam, Professor?"

"Once or twice, I have doubled the dose," I replied. "It's still harmless."

"You testified that you took no Temazepam the night of May twenty-fourth. Don't you take it every night?"

"No."

"I have here," Rudge said to the judge, "copies of two sequential prescriptions for Temazepam, written for Professor Goldman, one, a month after the other, each for thirty capsules. I would like to enter them as evidence." He handed them to the judge, who then handed them to the clerk.

"Might I see them?" I asked.

The clerk passed them to me. One was for May 4th, 1996, and the other for June 4th, 1996. I gave them back to the clerk.

"Here, Professor Goldman, I have two prescriptions for Temazepam thirty days apart. Obviously, you took one each night, is that not so?"

"Obviously not," I replied. "I go to the doctor for a prescription when I can. I go to the drugstore when I can. If I have a few extra capsules, this does not concern me. I find it reassuring."

"And you still insist that you did not take Temazepam on the night of May twenty-fourth?"

"That is correct."

"I have no more questions for this witness," Rudge said.

I left the witness stand and returned to my seat in the audience. Liz turned from her seat at the table, looking at me longingly. I had lied under oath, and it would be false to say that I did this with no compunctions. I had always taken my oath as an officer of the court very seriously; it was ingrained, you might say, as part of my nervous system and I thought of the lectures on legal ethics that I gave to every class I taught. Well, from here on, the case was Sarah's, with the assistance of J. J.—but then it had always been Sarah's. A man who has spent thirty years teaching contract law is neither a litigator nor a responsible criminal defender, and he does not become one overnight.

The next witness Sarah called was Dr. Sam Bernstein. His doctorate was in inorganic chemistry, and he worked in the forensics department of Manhattan South. She asked the judge whether she might treat him as a hostile witness. It was he who had analyzed and matched the lipstick on the fax paper with Autumn. He was a small, pink-cheeked man with a Vandyke and a mustache, and his attitude immediately bespoke a long history of testimony.

"Dr. Bernstein," Sarah said, "what is your work at Manhattan South?"

"Chemical analysis."

"Do you mean in the broadest sense? Not a single specialty?"

"I am available for any matter that requires chemical analysis. Of course, I have assistants."

"But in the case of the murder of William Sedgwick Hopper, you undertook the analysis of the lipstick writing on the fax paper yourself. Is that not so?"

"Yes. When dealing with important cases, specifically in homicides, I do the work myself. With assistance when I require it."

"Now, can you tell me how many substances—

that is, chemical ingredients—are involved in the manufacture of lipstick in the United States?"

"I'm afraid not."

"Why not?"

"Because there are so many chemical ingredients that I could only make a guess."

"I don't want a guess, thank you. Nevertheless, you made an analysis and Mr. Rudge entered your analysis as evidence for the state in this trial, the outcome of which could mean life imprisonment for the woman involved. Will you please tell me how you made this analysis?"

"I matched eleven chemical ingredients and then I matched the color."

"Does that mean you matched every chemical ingredient?"

"No. We do not work that way. I consider a match of eleven ingredients and color enough to draw a valid conclusion."

"Do you, indeed? And yet you know that this case depends on a series of pieces of circumstantial evidence, among which the lipstick match is very important. Do you, as a doctor of inorganic chemistry, consider your conclusion valid that Autumn, manufactured by Devlon, was the kind of lipstick used to write the words on the fax paper? Specifically, the kind of lipstick found in Mrs. Hopper's bag and in her bathroom?"

"Yes, I do."

"Would you please name the eleven ingredients upon which you depended?"

Bernstein, apparently expecting this question, took a small notebook from his jacket pocket and read: "Castor oil, acetylated lanolin, ozokerite, candelilla wax, paraffin, carnauba oil, cetyl alcohol, mica, cyclomethicone, synthetic wax, and lanolin. And, of course, color."

"Thank you," Sarah said. "I have no more questions for this witness."

Rudge appeared to hesitate; then he rose and asked Bernstein how many years he had spent in police forensics.

"Twenty-nine, sir."

"And you have matched lipsticks previously?"

"Frequently."

"How frequently, if you can recall?"

"Taking twenty-nine years and including my staff, I would say over a hundred times."

"And how many times have you been challenged and proven wrong?"

"I have often been challenged but proven wrong only once. And that was a singular case of a European lip rouge. But that was in 1977, and our methods have improved since then."

"Then you have no doubt that the words on the

sheet of fax paper were written with a stick of Autumn lipstick, the same brand of lipstick that was found in the bag of Mrs. Hopper and the second stick that was found in her bedroom?"

"None whatsoever. I would stake my professional career on it."

"That is all," Rudge said. "Thank you."

The judge then looked inquiringly at Sarah, but she spread her hands and shook her head.

"You may step down," Kilpatrick said to Bernstein.

Sarah's next witness gave his name as Leland Greene, took the oath, and identified himself as chief chemist for Household Research Laboratories. He was a dark-skinned man with bushy eyebrows and black suspicious eyes.

"Would you tell us the nature of your work?" Sarah asked.

"Household Research analytically checks products produced for household use, and their effect on human beings. We do not deal with medications, except for certain topical preparations. For the most part, we deal with products for household and garden use. Also, foods when the packager desires to know the caloric and vitamin content."

"And among these products you analyze, are there lipsticks?"

"Oh, yes."

"Now you will recall that I gave you a piece of fax paper, on which three letters were printed with lipstick. Is that not so?"

"Yes."

"And I asked you to compare them with Autumn and to tell me whether they were identical and whether the Autumn had been used to write the large block letters on the fax paper. Is that not so?"

"Yes, it is."

"And you made the comparison, did you not?"

"Yes, we established the comparison."

"And are you ready now, under oath, to testify that the same brand of lipstick was used in both cases, in the printing and in the Autumn."

"No, I can't testify to that."

Suddenly, their was a buzz among the reporters, and the jurors' attention visibly intensified.

"Why not? Will you please explain why you can't testify that both lipsticks were the same?"

"Simply, madam, because there is no way to prove that they were the same. Devlon's Autumn is an excellent product, the result of years of experiment that few of the smaller companies can afford. It contains elements of seventeen substances in varying amounts, aside from the color elements. Devlon may patent this lipstick, but by varying the amounts of each ingredient, the patent can be circumscribed. In a sense, all lipsticks are essentially the same, and while I was able to find trace amounts of each substance in the paper you gave me to work with, it was impossible to determine the exact proportions."

"May I show the witness the entire sheet of paper that was entered into evidence, Your Honor?" Sarah asked the judge.

"Yes, of course."

The clerk handed Sarah the sheet of fax paper, restored in full now, and she passed it on to Greene, and asked him to look at it.

"If you had the entire sheet, would an exact analysis be possible?"

"Perhaps we could come closer to an exact analysis, but it would still be impossible to determine the amount of each ingredient. There are over a hundred lipsticks produced in America that have the same ingredients as Autumn—or at least 90 percent of these ingredients."

"And what about color? Can the color of Autumn be replicated?"

"Very easily. It is a 'lake' color. Lake is a category of colors. At least eight other companies produce lipstick of the same tint as Autumn. This color category has been in use for at least a hundred years. There is no way to restrict its use."

"Now, Dr. Greene, earlier, a chemist who works for the New York City police department matched the lipstick found in Ms. Hopper's purse with—"

Rudge was on his feet, angrily objecting, as Sarah said, "with the printing on the fax paper."

"Calls for an opinion!" Rudge snapped.

"But if a physician," Kilpatrick said mildly, "testified to the life or death of a subject, that would also call for an opinion, would it not?"

"He's not a physician."

"Come, come, Mr. Rudge. He is a chemist and, therefore an expert witness so I am going to overrule your objection and allow Ms. Morton to complete her question and the witness to answer it. This is a capital case."

Sarah said, "This chemist from police forensics found eleven substances that were identical on both the fax paper and in the lipstick. What do you think of his decision that it was Autumn?"

Again Rudge objected, and Kilpatrick sustained the objection. "Phrase it differently, Ms. Morton."

"Is such a conclusion valid?" Sarah asked.

"Not in our laboratory. Of course, we are not a police forensic laboratory."

Rudge objected and demanded that the last phrase be stricken. The judge sustained the objection and ordered the jury to disregard the witness's last statement.

"Do you have with you, Dr. Greene," Sarah asked, almost coyly, "some lipsticks that might readily be mistaken for Devlon's Autumn?"

Taking three lipsticks out of his jacket pocket, Greene held them up for the jury to see. "I have only three. You asked me to bring only three."

"May they be entered as evidence, Your Honor?" Sarah asked. Greene handed the lipsticks to the judge, who examined them curiously, manipulating them so that the contents might be seen, and then handed them to Rudge, who couldn't wait to get his hands on them. While he was examining them, Sarah said, "I asked you to bring only three to avoid confusion here in court. If I had asked for half a dozen, could you have found them?"

"Yes, but it would have cost you a lot more," Greene replied, and while the court and the jury broke into laughter, Rudge objected strenuously and the judge sustained him.

I could see that Kilpatrick was struck by Sarah. Like many intelligent women, Sarah grew on people. There is a mind-set among many people, whether they admit it or not, that women are inferior in intelligence. Sarah was not only tall, lissome, and good-looking but she managed Mr. Rudge with ease, knowing exactly how to use him and cause him to explode with objections. Bit by bit, she was tearing his case to shreds.

"Now suppose," she said to Greene, "that the message on the fax paper had been written by any one of these four lipsticks, to include Autumn. Is there any way it could have been proven that Autumn was the writing instrument?"

Kilpatrick called Sarah up to the bench after Rudge exploded with an objection. "You are trying my patience," he whispered to her—as she told me later. "You know better."

She walked over to the jury box, sighed while not facing the judge, and said to Greene, "The three lipsticks are identical to Autumn in color and composition, are they not?"

"They are."

"Can you prove that?"

"Only to the extent of my company's reputation for truth and integrity. Here are three bonded statements—" He took three folded sheets out of his pocket. "By bonded, Ms. Morton, I mean that we stand behind every analysis with a cash payment double our retainer."

"May I offer them as evidence?"

"Certainly," Greene said, handing them to Rudge, who looked through them and then passed them to the judge.

"How many substances does each contain?"

"Seventeen and the coloring."

"Are the amounts equal to Autumn—I mean the seventeen substances used in the lipstick—that is, each amount?"

"No, they vary slightly. But in the lipstick on the paper, there was no way for us to make such a precise determination."

"Did you make the attempt?"

"Of course. We have state-of-the-art instruments."

"Thank you, Dr. Greene." And to the judge, she said, "I have no more questions for this witness, Your Honor."

"Will you cross-examine, Mr. Rudge?" Kilpatrick asked.

"Yes, Your Honor." Rudge approached Greene, and both men regarded each other without pleasure. "Dr. Greene," Rudge said, "have you ever visited the forensic laboratory of the police precinct we call Manhattan South?"

"No."

"Then you can have no opinion of the quality of their work or what instruments they use—is that not so?"

"Yes. All I know is that in this case—"

"You have answered the question. Now tell me, could the sample on fax paper that was given to you be Autumn by Devlon?"

"Well, sir—"

"Either yes or no!" Rudge snapped.

"Yes. It is possible."

"I have no other questions of this witness," Rudge

said. All through this, as all through the trial so far, his fellow prosecutor, Helen Slater, had sat in silence, making copious notes on her pad.

Judge Kilpatrick now announced a break for lunch and said that court would convene again at one forty-five.

Liz threw her arms around me and kissed me and whispered Sarah was wonderful, wasn't she? and that now there was some hope. Then the media swooped down on us, and we had to push our way through to get out of the courthouse and keep our lips locked, as we had all agreed. But Sarah answered a single question: "What do you think your chances are?"

"We will win because our client is innocent."

She still used *we* but shook her head and refused to say a word when asked whether I was still her associate and why I was sitting on a back bench. Rudge was willing to talk, and that gave us a chance to escape. We walked to a small restaurant on the edge of Chinatown and ate heartily of roast pork, dumplings, Chinese vegetables, and fried rice. Sarah shook off our congratulations, reminding us that we still had the gun. "Oh, Ike," she said, "what possessed you to buy a gun twenty years ago, I'll never know. It's a white man's shtick. A couple of blacks move into the neighborhood, and, lo and behold, everybody owns a gun."

"Sarah, Sarah," Liz said, "you were wonderful, and how did Ike know twenty years ago that I would come

into his life? If it weren't me, it would be Ike as the accused."

"I wasn't wonderful, and the whole thing's on a
string—and a very thin string, at that. I feel that I'm
throwing dice with Liz's life." When Liz's face fell, Sarah
said quickly, "Damn it, no. We're going to win. We have
to."

"I think I would prefer to die rather than spend the
rest of my life in prison," Liz said, and that brought a
voluminous outcry of protest from J. J., who had come
to divide her worship between Sarah and Liz. J. J. was a
smart young woman, with close-cropped curly hair
and a round face, and two small children left behind by
a vanished husband. Every day at four o'clock, until
the trial had begun, Liz took off with J. J. to pick up the
kids and deliver them to J. J.'s mother. Between them
they were working out a plan to lure Sarah out of being a public defender. J. J. had enough assorted credits
from Hunter College that, with the influence I could
bring to bear, she could enter Columbia Law. Then
Sarah would open a law office and J. J. would work
with her. Liz was an enthusiastic supporter of the
scheme. It was not until the trial began that I realized
how much of an innocent Elizabeth truly was, innocent in a world that was not shaped to bear out anything she had been taught.

When we returned to court, fifteen minutes early,
the clerk informed us that Judge Kilpatrick wished to

see Sarah and Rudge in chambers. Kilpatrick began by noting that Liz was her last witness. "I told you," he said, "that it troubles me for the accused to take the stand. I have been thinking about it. Do you intend to claim the 'battered-woman syndrome'?"

"No, Your Honor," Sarah replied. "That would mean an admission of guilt. She will testify to her innocence."

"I am still troubled."

"I trust, Your Honor, that you will give me some leeway."

"I find such a question totally improper."

Rudge angrily agreed with the judge.

Sarah shrugged. "I apologize. It was stupid of me."

Kilpatrick's reaction was annoyance, but Sarah felt she had accomplished what she had intended. She came out of the judge's chambers and whispered to me, "God help me, Ike, I'm shooting craps with Liz's life."

"I trust you." What else could I say?

The courtroom was filling up, and a minute or two later, the clerk called out for everybody to rise. Judge Kilpatrick took his place on the bench, and now I looked at him as if I had never seen him before— looked at him newly. Liz was the last witness that Sarah would call, and possibly sometime this afternoon or tomorrow morning, the die would be cast. Much of how it might be cast would depend on that stern, lean-faced, bespectacled man on the bench.

But for now, Sarah called Jerry Brown. Wearing knife-edge taupe twill trousers and a blue jacket, white shirt with a thin blue stripe, and a hand-tied bow tie, he came off more as a fashion model out of *Gentleman's Quarterly* than as Hollywood's notion of a private investigator. He took his place on the witness stand, nodded ingratiatingly to the jury, and eased his trousers just a trifle. He took the oath and then gave his name as Jerome Brown and his profession as private investigator.

"How long have you been a private investigator?" Sarah asked him.

"Twelve years, ma'am."

"Are you licensed by the police?"

"Yes, Ms. Morton."

"And you were engaged by Professor Goldman to work on the defense of Elizabeth Hopper?"

"That is correct."

"Briefly, what did that work consist of?"

"A trip to Boston, checking police and hospital records, and certain work here in New York City."

"I am interested in your local work for Professor Goldman, here in the city. I understand that you have written a statement of your work, and have had it sworn and notarized."

Rudge rose to object, and the judge asked Sarah,

"Where is the statement, Ms. Morton? Do you intend to enter it as evidence?"

Sarah went to the table, took a folder, and gave it to Kilpatrick. Rudge asked to approach.

"I intend to cover the same material in my questioning of the witness," Sarah explained.

"Then why this statement?" Rudge demanded.

Sarah shrugged. "It's part of his report. I felt I should enter it as evidence."

"A bit odd, but why not?" Kilpatrick said. "However, we'll hold it until he testifies."

Sarah went back to Jerry Brown, "Mr. Brown, would you describe the work you did for us in New York?"

"Yes. It was based on the police case. Professor Goldman stated that Mrs. Hopper had come to bed with him at nine-thirty. The police speculated that Hopper had been dead for some hours before his corpse was discovered at about midnight. Manhattan South forensics reduced the time to between one and two hours. By that kind of thinking, he was killed between ten and eleven."

Rudge rose to object, and Kilpatrick said, "All of this is connected. You can cross-examine, Mr. Rudge." He turned to Brown. "Please go on, Mr. Brown."

"Thank you, Your Honor," Brown said. "My objective was to check the travel time from Professor Goldman's apartment and the Omnibus Building. Now, between nine and eleven P.M., there are two hours. I left Professor Goldman's apartment building at nine P.M., by the basement, and walked out to the Drive after wedging the basement door. I found a cab on Riverside Drive. I took the cab down to Wall Street and the Omnibus Building. There was little traffic at that hour, and we made it to the Omnibus Building in forty-one minutes. Eleven minutes had passed before I hailed the cab, and I allowed thirty minutes for the supposed murderer to do what was supposed to have been done, which includes getting up to Hopper's office and then back to the entranceway. This, of course, presupposes that the cleaning crew had left the door to the building open or that Hopper was there to open it. The cab was waiting, and I told the driver to get back to Professor Goldman's apartment as fast as he could. But the traffic was heavier, and it took him forty-three minutes. I have here a notarized statement from the cab driver with the time included. Total, one hundred and twenty-five minutes, or thirty-five minutes more than the police estimate."

The people's case rested almost entirely on Liz having ample time to go down to Wall Street and back.

Rudge rose to object, claiming that Brown's whole performance was ridiculous, not only hearsay but based entirely on the evidence I had just given. Kilpatrick called the lawyers to the bench.

As Sarah told me afterwards, Kilpatrick said to

Rudge, "You had the opportunity to cross-examine Professor Goldman."

"Your Honor, the man's in love with the woman. His testimony is worthless."

"Let the jury decide that, Mr. Rudge. If you wish to bring charges against him for perjury, you are free to do so, providing you have some proof of his perjury. Meanwhile, your objection is overruled."

Then Sarah asked Brown if he had questioned the police about checking whether any cabs had taken a passenger from 115th Street to Wall Street and back.

"Manhattan South took care of that. They came up with nothing. I had that information from Captain Rudley, chief of detectives at Manhattan South."

"I am sure that Mr. Rudge had the same information," Sarah said.

"Ms. Morton!" Kilpatrick exploded.

"Please, Your Honor, forgive me." She appeared the proper, chastised attorney. "Now Mr. Brown," she went on, "I instructed you to make the same journey to Wall Street with all speed, taking the subway. Did you do so?"

"I did."

"And what was your time?"

"I started out at nine P.M. from Professor Goldman's apartment building. Using the same time interval at the Omnibus Building, the trip took two hours and ten minutes. Trains run less frequently at that hour."

"Then, in your opinion, Mr. Brown, is there any possibility that Mrs. Hopper could have killed Mr. Hopper?"

Rudge was on his feet, enraged at this kind of call for a conclusion, but already Kilpatrick had instructed Brown not to answer the question.

"Now, Mr. Brown," Sarah said, "did you call the Boston Financial Corporation where Mr. Hopper worked and ask what their familiar name for Mr. Hopper was?"

"Yes, ma'am."

"And their answer, Mr. Brown?"

"Sedge. They all called him Sedge."

"And did you go to the Cambridge Country Club, where Mr. Hopper was a member, and ask the golf pro the same question?"

"I did."

"And the golf pro's answer, Mr. Brown?"

"Sedge—they all called him Sedge."

At this point, Rudge rose and protested that this was all hearsay.

Judge Kilpatrick took a long moment, and then he said, "I am going to allow it, Mr. Rudge. It goes to a very important point on the part of the defense. They hired a private investigator and sent him to Boston. You can cover the same territory with a series of telephone calls. Mr. Brown is testifying under oath. If you can prove otherwise, you can bring in other witnesses to support you. This is a capital case, and I am inclined to allow Mr. Brown's testimony to go into the record."

Grudgingly, Rudge nodded; then whispered to Ms. Slater, who left the court.

"For some months, when she lived in Boston, Mrs. Hopper employed a maid, Agatha Jones by name. I instructed you to track her down and speak to her. Did you?"

"Yes, I did."

"And did you ask her whether she ever heard anyone call Mr. Hopper Billy?"

"I did. Her answer was no. Everyone she heard called him Sedge."

Sarah spread her hands. "I have no other questions for this witness."

"Cross-examine?" the judge asked.

Angry now, Rudge asked that my testimony be read back. Then he said to Brown, "Mr. Brown, you base your testimony on Professor Goldman's testimony. Have you any other source for his statement that he went to bed at nine and Mrs. Hopper got into the same bed at nine-thirty on the night of the murder?"

"No. Only his own, and what Mrs. Hopper told me."

"Then everything you have described here is based on the testimony of the accused and her lover?"

"Yes, on Professor Goldman's testimony. The accused has not testified yet to my knowledge."

"And all your meandering journeys between Wall Street and 115th Street are based on pure hearsay, or at the worst, perjury—"

Sarah sprang to her feet, the first time during the trial that I had seen her lose her temper. She cried out, "This, Your Honor, is too much. Not only is Mr. Rudge calling for a conclusion, but without cause or reason or a shred of proof, he is charging Professor Goldman with perjury!"

"Approach!" Kilpatrick said, angry himself, and— as Sarah told me later—he whispered coldly to Rudge, "You sir, had weeks to prepare for this trial. If you had a shred of evidence that Professor Goldman is committing perjury, you would have known this during discovery. You have a reputation for preparing a case properly. It appears to me that you were woefully deficient."

"I had no knowledge that he would be a witness."

"But you had knowledge that Mrs. Hopper would be a witness and that she would testify to the same thing. You could have called for a recess and then added to the discovery."

Then the attorneys went back to their tables and

Kilpatrick instructed the jury to ignore the remarks of Mr. Rudge.

Rudge said, "I have no other questions for this witness."

Like Kilpatrick, I was astonished at Rudge's sloppiness. It occurred to me that possibly he was caught between the rock and the hard place they talk about today—his desire to win the case against his need for the large black vote in Brooklyn. Fortunately for us, that could very well have thrown him off balance.

Jerry Brown, refraining from smiling, straightened his jacket, rose, and left the stand.

The clerk called for Mrs. Elizabeth Hopper, and Liz took her place on the stand, stated her name, and took the oath.

Sarah rose and faced her. "Mrs. Hopper, did you kill William Sedgwick Hopper, your divorced husband?"

"No, I did not," Liz replied.

"I have no other questions," Sarah said, returning to the table.

There was a gasp of disbelief from the audience, a buzz of excitement from the press section, and an expression of utter bewilderment on the faces of some of the jurors. Kilpatrick was studying Sarah intently, but only said, "Cross-examine, Mr. Rudge."

Rudge, too, had glanced at Sarah warily. I wondered afterwards whether he had any notion of Sarah's play and risk; but whether he did or not, he could not forbear to question Liz.

She was very calm, her face placid; I was far from placid. I have never had a heart attack, but this was close.

Rudge rose and said, "Your Honor, I have here in my hand a bill of record from Dr. Alvin C. Cohen, a dental surgeon residing at 16 Apple Street in Boston. I wish to enter it as evidence."

Kilpatrick took a long moment, and then he said to Sarah, "Are you going to object, Ms. Morton?"

"No, Your Honor. I see no reason why it should not be entered as evidence."

Again, Kilpatrick took a long moment before he spoke. "Mr. Rudge, how are you going to connect this?"

"It goes to motive, Your Honor." Then he turned and glanced curiously at Sarah.

"You may enter it as evidence," Kilpatrick said.

Rudge handed the paper to the clerk, who marked it and then returned it to Rudge, who handed it to Liz.

"Do you recognize this paper, Mrs. Hopper?"

"Yes, of course."

"Would you explain to the jury what it is."

"It's a copy of a bill sent to my then husband, William Hopper, by Dr. Alvin Cohen. The bill was for seven thousand dollars—for four front teeth, implants, and replacements."

"Mrs. Hopper, an implant is a titanium post placed in a hole drilled in the jawbone, upon which a new tooth is fixed. Is that not so?"

"Yes, that is so."

"Would you tell the jury the circumstances that led to the loss of those four teeth?"

The judge held up his hand and beckoned the lawyers to the bench. "I will not have a mistrial," he whispered to Sarah. "This is all new ground."

"It goes to motive," Rudge argued.

"God forbid we should have a mistrial," Sarah said. "Your Honor, I have no objection to the question or the answer."

All this was conveyed to me later. I saw the judge bite his lip and nod.

"I'll repeat my question," Rudge said, but the enthusiasm had gone out of his voice. He was beginning to realize, I believe, that Sarah was playing his hand; but just how she was playing it he certainly did not know.

"What were the circumstances that led up to this?"

"We had been married two years and I had not conceived. Children were very important to him, as they were to me. He forced me to be examined by a gynecologist, and the report was that I would never be able to conceive. He went into a rage when he read that report, and completely lost his temper. He accused me of deliberately deceiving him. I lost the teeth from a blow to my mouth from his clenched fist. He wore two rings on his right fist and that split both my lips. I had to have cosmetic surgery as well as tooth replacement, and that cost more than eighteen thousand dollars. I felt guilty about costing him all that money. He apologized, and I forgave him."

"And you never held him responsible?"

"Sedge had a terrible temper."

"You haven't answered the question."

"I couldn't hold Sedge responsible for his temper. He was a sick man."

"Did you hate him?" Rudge persisted.

"No. I guess I pitied him."

I think that at this point Rudge knew he was being used, and rather than step deeper into the trap, he decided to wait for the redirect. "I have no more questions for this witness."

Kilpatrick had been following this closely, making notes through it, and instead of suggesting that Liz step down, he turned to Sarah with a very thin smile—just a crinkling at the corners of his mouth, but the closest thing to a smile since the trial began.

"Redirect, Ms. Morton?"

"Yes, Your Honor."

"Your witness," Rudge said peevishly.

"Mrs. Hopper," Sarah asked, almost casually, "what did you call your ex-husband, Mr. William Sedgwick Hopper?"

Rudge objected, saying that this had no place in the redirect.

"I'll connect it, if you please, Your Honor," Sarah said.

"I'll allow it," Kilpatrick agreed. "I see no reason why not."

"I called him Sedge," Liz answered.

"I bring this up," Sarah said, "because in response to two previous questions, you called him Sedge. I find that odd. My question hinges on that. Since his name was William Sedgwick Hopper, how was it you never called him Billy or Bill?"

"No. No one called him Billy or Bill. I was introduced to him as Sedge."

Rudge objected as Liz spoke. Kilpatrick shook his head and said, "She said she would connect it, and she did."

"Did anyone ever call him Billy to your knowledge?"

"No."

"And his business associates in Boston? What did they call him familiarly?"

"Sedge. Everyone called him Sedge."

"Did you ever hear anyone call him Billy?"

"No, never."

"Now, we'll go to Mr. Rudge's question about your teeth," Sarah said, her tone dulcet. "This brutal attack took place after you were married two years. Before that, was there any physical abuse of you by Mr. Hopper?"

Reluctantly, Liz replied, "Only once. He came home late and he must have had a bad day. I think it was my fault. I tried to kiss him, and he was in no mood to be kissed. He hit me several times with his open hands. I don't think he meant to hurt me, but I was frightened and I ran into the bathroom. He was a very strong man, and I was frightened. There was a telephone in the bathroom and I called 911. When the police came, I refused to press any charges. He was a different man when he lost his temper. The police were agreeable; they still respected him as a great Olympic athlete."

Rudge rose and asked the judge whether we were to hear a biographical history of her married life in response to every question.

"She is trying to answer Ms. Morton's questions, Mr. Rudge. This is a capital case, and Ms. Morton has called only four witnesses. I think we can afford to be patient."

Sarah went to the table and selected a paper. "This is a copy of a bill from Massachusetts General Hospital for setting a broken arm and an overnight stay," she said to the jury. She turned to Kilpatrick. "May I enter it as evidence, Your Honor?"

"Yes, of course."

"This broken arm, Mrs. Hopper, how did it come about?"

"Well—must I?"

"I'm afraid you must. You have taken the oath and you have taken the witness stand of your own free will. I explained to you that under our law, here in America, you could not be forced to give testimony against yourself. I know this is terribly humiliating, but you must answer my questions."

Rudge was on his feet objecting. Irritated now, Kilpatrick said, "You opened this door, Mr. Rudge, and left it wide open. This trial would go better if you didn't object to whatever flies in. Your objection is overruled."

"Well, I'll try to explain," Liz said reluctantly—and I was amazed at how sincere this dialogue was, considering that it had been rehearsed. Well, Sarah had said that criminal trial was theater and after the endless spectacle of O. J. Simpson's trial, I was only too ready to believe her. Still, I was surprised at Liz's control.

"You see," Liz said, "he called me a liar constantly. It was his way of putting me down and breaking my spirit. I had run short on my allowance because I was moved one Sunday by our priest's sermon and I had put fifty dollars into the poor box. When I told him that—I hadn't intended to tell him, but when I did— he said I was lying; and when I stuck to my story, he twisted my arm. He said he would make me tell the truth this time, and—well, he broke my arm. I was crying from the pain, so he took me to Massachusetts General."

Sarah nodded, walked to the table, and picked up a batch of papers that were clipped together. Then she walked to face the jury, made eye contact with them, looked at the batch of papers, and made eye contact again. There was a black woman on the jury whose face was contorted with pain. I wondered what her life had been like. There was a man whose face was so dark and angry that I thought, if he'd had the opportunity, he would have dispatched William Hopper himself.

Then Sarah turned and said to the judge, "Here I have eleven police reports from two Boston precincts, each one a record of a 911 call by Elizabeth Hopper. In each case, she refused to bring charges. May I enter them as evidence, Your Honor?"

She handed them to Kilpatrick, who went through them, and then they were entered and handed to Rudge, who studied them with a blank face and then handed them to Sarah, who gave them to Liz.

"I have given you eleven police reports of calls to the police for assistance. Would you look at each of them?"

Liz did as instructed. There was a hush in the courtroom during this time. When Liz had finished looking at them, Sarah handed them to the clerk.

"Are they all valid? You mentioned one incident. Are all of these valid?"

"Yes." Her voice was a whisper.

"Please speak up," the judge said.

"Yes," Liz repeated, but louder.

"Why didn't you mention them?" Sarah asked.

"I was so ashamed."

"And why were you so ashamed?"

"Because I stayed until he divorced me. I married late, in my thirties. I was educated in a convent school. I was taught that marriage was indissoluble and I believed it."

"Tell me, Mrs. Hopper, did your husband—your ex-husband—did he belong to the National Rifle Association?"

Rudge rose to object. The judge intervened and asked Sarah, "Where are going with this, Ms. Morton? It appears to me that you're way out in left field."

"I will connect it. It goes to motive, Your Honor."

"Does it?" To Rudge he said, "I'll let her answer it, Mr. Rudge."

"You have my objection."

"I said I'll let her answer it. Overruled."

Rudge grimaced angrily.

"You may answer the question," the judge told Liz.

"Yes, he did."

"Did he have a gun?"

"Yes, he had a number of guns. He had two automatic pistols. He kept one in his night table and another downstairs. He also had two shotguns, which he used for duck hunting, and two hunting rifles."

"Did he enjoy hunting?"

"Yes. He made me go with him. I tried to get out of it, but he got very angry. He taught me to use the shotguns and the pistols. He said that in this world, one couldn't survive without a gun."

"Did he keep the guns loaded?"

"Yes, always. He kept them in a glass case in his study."

"Did he keep the pistols loaded?"

"Yes. He once said that the time it took to load a gun could mean the difference between life and death."

"Then you always had loaded guns at hand—how long were you married?"

"Eight years."

"And when you went hunting, where would you go?"

"He had his own duck blind, in Maine, on a lake."

"What do you mean by a 'duck blind'?"

"A wooden platform and shelter, sort of camouflaged, at the edge of a lake, where you wait for the ducks. I hated it. I couldn't kill a duck, and even to watch him do it was awful."

"But you could kill him and say it was an accident, couldn't you?" Sarah said.

"Oh, my God, no! No!"

"But you have told us that you had eight years of what might be regarded as pure hell, didn't you? And there you were, sitting next to him with a loaded shotgun, and all you had to do was to pull the trigger and then say it was an accident—"

I was watching Rudge as he half rose from his seat to object—and then he dropped back. He still didn't know where this was going.

Liz was in tears now. "How can you ask me such a thing?" This had not been rehearsed.

"Because it's my role to ask the questions and yours to answer them. Will you please answer the question, Mrs. Hopper."

"Do you want a recess?" Kilpatrick asked Sarah.

Liz shook her head, and a recess at this moment was the last thing Sarah desired. Liz wiped away the tears and assured the judge that she was all right.

"I think my client can answer the question," Sarah said. "Why didn't you kill your husband? Eleven times you had to call the police. He knocked out your front teeth, smashed your face, broke your arm, and beat you again and again. Why didn't you kill him when you had such an easy and safe opportunity?"

"This kind of hypothetical question certainly calls for a conjecture," Kilpatrick said. "Mr. Rudge has not seen fit to object. Do you intend to continue in this direction?"

"I have introduced nothing," Sarah replied. "Everything has been introduced as evidence, some of it by the people. Her state of mind certainly goes to the facts."

"Very well. If Mr. Rudge has no objections, she may answer the question."

Liz had pulled herself together. "Because I would have to answer before God," she said softly.

"Would you speak up," Kilpatrick said. "I don't think the jury heard you."

"Because I would have to answer to God," Liz said firmly.

A black woman and another woman on the jury, a white woman, were wiping away their own tears.

"What was your state of mind during the years of your marriage?"

"I was broken," Liz said. "My heart and mind and soul."

Rudge objected to this, but the judge said that since he had allowed what had proceeded it, he would allow this as well. He overruled the objection.

"I asked you why you didn't leave him."

"My vows were my vows. That never changed."

"Why didn't he leave you?"

"He would have, but he wanted an annulment. He could not inherit from his father if he were divorced without an annulment."

"Why didn't you leave him in Boston, Mrs. Hopper?"

"Because there was nothing left of *me*. He had crushed everything in me. I was incapable of leaving, of doing anything of my own will. He had called me a liar so often, beaten me so often with words as well as fists, told me I was worthless so often that I believed him. And there were the other women, one woman after another, and he never failed to tell me how superior they were to me. Where would I go? I believed him."

Rudge was on his feet, objecting and asking whether we had to listen to a psychological history of her state of mind.

"She answered the question, Mr. Rudge," Kilpatrick said mildly.

"Did he get the annulment, Mrs. Hopper?"

"Yes, in New York, and then the divorce."

"Why did he move to New York, Mrs. Hopper?"

"Some clients in Boston raised questions about his methods. He got an offer from a Wall Street firm, and he accepted it."

"And you went with him to New York?"

"Yes. I had already accepted a new teaching job in the art department at Marymount College. I thought I could start a new life in a new place. I really hoped I could speed up the annulment and divorce if I came to New York, too. At that point, all I wanted was the annulment and the divorce—and then never to see him again."

"And since you met Professor Goldman, have you ever seen Mr. Hopper?"

"No!"

"Do you love Professor Goldman?"

"He gave me life and hope when I had no life and no hope. I love him more than I can say."

"I will ask you again, and I will ask you to remember that you are under oath, an oath taken before God. Did you kill William Sedgwick Hopper?"

"No, I did not."

"I have no other questions for this witness."

"Mr. Rudge?" the judge asked.

Rudge shook his head.

"Then we will adjourn until tomorrow—unless you wish to call a witness—either you, Ms. Morton, or the people."

Rudge and Sarah replied in the negative, and the judge asked them to be ready to deliver their closing statements the following day.

We left the court as usual, pushing our way through the cluster of media people and cameras, and found a cab to take us uptown. At this point I felt certain that we would get either a hung jury or an acquittal. But as Sarah had said often, in a capital case there is no certainty. She had played her cards as she saw them, laid them out with all her skill, rehearsed every possible question and answer for weeks—with only one end in mind, to win the case. I was unsure whether or not I had perjured myself; whether Liz had I did not know, and I had no intention of asking her. Much would depend on the closing statements, and Sarah said that she and J. J. would go on to her office for some last-minute work on her closing. We were a somber group, and now that the witnesses had been heard, no one appeared willing to talk about it.

Sarah dropped us off at my apartment. There were no more secrets. We were public figures and would remain so for a goodly time to come, as Gregory, the doorman, underlined by wishing us luck and hoping that it had gone well today.

I suggested to Liz that we might go out for dinner later, but she shook her head. "I wish it weren't too warm for a fire," she said. "I was thinking all day how good it would be to sit in front of the fire and just curl up to you, Ike, and pretend that there was no world outside, and perhaps look at the river as the sun sets. I would feel safe."

"You are safe."

"No, dear man. I will always be that woman accused of murdering her divorced husband. That will never change. Wherever I go, they'll look at me and say, that's Elizabeth Hopper."

"Well, they might say, that's Elizabeth Goldman."

"You still would?"

"I still will, and you must eat something. We can

go to that Chinese restaurant over on Broadway where no one will know us. You've had an awful day."

"It was not so awful. Sarah and I rehearsed it until I was answering questions in my sleep. She knew every question and every answer. She even knew which jurors would cry. I never thought that a trial could be anything like this."

"But you didn't rehearse your tears."

"No. They were real. They came from remembering. Memory is a terrible thing, Ike."

"But without it, we wouldn't be human, would we?"

"No, I guess not."

"And will you come out to that Chinese place, and we'll order Peking Duck?"

"Oh, no. Don't make me eat, Ike. I know it's a thought of love, but don't tonight. Open a bottle of wine and put out some crackers, and we'll just sit and watch the sunset and get a little tight, and then go to bed, and I'll take one of those sleeping pills that they made such a fuss over and I'll fall asleep in your arms."

And that's what we did, and she fell asleep with her warm body against mine.

CHAPTER TEN

The Summation

At about four a.m. the following morning, Liz awakened, whimpering with fear; and when I took her in my arms and quieted her, she told me that she had a nightmare, so real that she could not shake it off. In her dream, she was in prison—an old, withered, white-haired woman, who had just been told that her parole had been denied and she would have to die in prison.

"Ike," she said, "it was so terrible and real. Everything was real, not like in a dream. I saw the little drops of water condensing on the stone walls of my cell, and I wore a gray prison dress that was torn and tattered. People say you dream of the future, that what you dream will happen. But Ike, you won't let it happen—

oh, Ike, I've been rotten for you. I've dumped on you and dumped on you, and given you nothing but trouble."

"Liz, baby, I used to dream that I had sprouted wings and I could fly, but I'm still walking around on these two old feet. A dream's a dream, nothing more. You're frightened, but it will all be over soon, and you'll be free, and we can go on with our plans. I get phone calls from my son asking whether I need money. I don't need money. I need you. Now it's half past four and the clock is set for seven. Let's get a few hours of sleep."

We both managed to fall asleep. The clock woke us at seven, and while Liz fixed breakfast, I turned on the TV. We were headline news, burnished with crayon portraits drawn by the network artists, none of them too flattering. Liz rebelled at the price of cab fare down to the tip of Manhattan. We took the subway, grateful that we were not recognized—but no one actually looks at anyone on the subway. J. J. and Sarah were already seated at the table when we got to court, which was almost full, still a half hour before Kilpatrick was expected. Liz took her seat at the table, and J. J. put her arms around her and kissed her and told her not to worry. Sarah looked bright and cheerful. "Jerry Brown came around last night. No matter how decisively you throw a man out, he still thinks he can come around for conjugal visits now and then. He was in court yesterday. He says it's a lead-pipe cinch, and he enjoys being on the winning team. I threw him out anyway."

"Except that he came back later with three big pizzas."

"You have a big mouth, J. J."

"I like him."

I took my place in the row behind them. Rudge came in with his silent assistant, doing Sarah the honor of nodding at her. There were more black people in the audience than I had ever seen in court before, due to a big story in the *Post* the day before, with Sarah's picture on the front of the paper. Precisely at ten, Kilpatrick came in and took his seat on the bench. The jury was already in the box, and a couple of photographers who had the temerity to photograph the judge as he entered evoked an angry response from him.

Then he tapped with his gavel and asked Sarah whether she was ready.

"Yes, Your Honor."

"I want absolute silence during the summations," the judge said. "There is to be no applause and no comment. Anyone who violates this will be ejected."

Sarah was dressed in a black sheath, with a bit of pink silk around her neck. "Good morning, ladies and gentlemen of the jury," she began in her deep, throaty voice. "There are summations that go on for hours, because there are cases of great complexity. I don't see this as a case of great complexity. The facts of this case are very simple, and they add up to a loose circle of circumstantial evidence. A murder was committed on May twenty-fourth of this year, in the Omnibus Building on Wall Street. You have listened to the details that the police presented. You have listened to the evidence of the detective sergeant in charge of the case. Briefly, a man named William Sedgwick Hopper was either working late or had an after-hours appointment with a person at his office. At some moment near ten o'clock, this person held a gun to the back of his head and killed him. Hopper, the murdered man, was in the process of writing a check for one hundred thousand dollars. The check was made out to cash, but Hopper died before he had an opportunity to sign his name to it, so the check is worthless. Then his killer tore a sheet of paper from the fax machine in Hopper's office and wrote on it, SWEET JOURNEY, BILLY. The killer then put the murder weapon on the sheet of fax paper and left.

"The New York Police could have called his former employer, the president of the Boston Investment Corp., who had a long and intimate acquaintance with William Sedgwick Hopper; and the police could have asked him by what name friends of Mr. Hopper called him. It seems to me that this would be one of the most important facts of this case, but they did not bother to make the call. We did. We made the call, and were told that at the Boston Investment Corporation, Mr. Hopper was known as Sedge. Mr. Brown spoke to the golf pro at the Cambridge Country Club, of which Mr. Hopper had been a member. The golf pro did not even know that Hopper's first name was William. He always called him Sedge, as did everyone else in the golfing circle.

"For some months, when she lived in Boston, Mrs. Hopper had employed a maid. Her name was Agatha Jones. By telephone inquiry, Mr. Brown found her address in Boston, and he spoke to her. She, too, confirmed the fact that she had never heard Mr. Hopper called anything but Sedge by a person familiar to him. This information was given to the police at the first precinct, but they evidently considered it of no importance. I consider it of the greatest importance. I ask you, members of the jury, why and how, at a moment of high excitement and after an act of murder, the perpetrator of the murder should suddenly use a name for the victim that he had never used. Why should Sedge become Billy? Perhaps I can answer that. My investigator, Jerome Brown, questioned a number of women who worked at Garson, Weeds and Anderson—all of them knew Mr. Hopper either as Mr. Hopper or Billy, as did a number of male members of the firm. I accuse no one, but I do wonder why the accused could make this sudden switch of familiar name.

"Now, let us see how the police went about deciding that Elizabeth Hopper, the defendant in this case, was none other than the killer: Their first bit of brilliant deduction led them to believe that the killer was a woman. Why? Two reasons: first, the note on the fax paper was written with a lipstick. Second, they decided that a man would never use the name Billy. A man doesn't call another man, named William, Billy. Effeminate! Not macho! He calls him Bill. I must add a third reason, women's intuition. A female police officer, Annabelle Schwartz, was present. Her intuition told her that the killer was a woman.

"Now let us follow the trail of evidence. The gun that killed Mr. Hopper was sitting right there on the piece of fax paper. It was registered to Professor Isaac Goldman. The killer may have had an IQ of about thirty; in any case, he made no attempt to test the intelligence of the detectives. He left the gun there, so that the cops could go directly to the residence of Professor Goldman. Elizabeth Hopper is the professor's fiancé. They were to be married the week after she was arrested. Professor Goldman had kept the gun in a drawer in his bedroom for many years. When the police went to look for it, it was missing, perhaps stolen. The detectives refused to believe that a stolen gun is sold and resold, though Detective Hull, in charge of the case, testified that a stolen gun travels from hand to hand. They also cast no suspicion on Professor Goldman. By then, three days after the crime, they had convinced themselves that the killer was a woman—and who better than Mrs. Hopper, who was then living with Professor Goldman? They buttressed this by finding, in her purse and in her bedroom, two lipsticks, both Devlon's Autumn. Meanwhile, the forensic lab at Manhattan South had determined that the note on the fax paper had also been written with Autumn lipstick.

"Professor Goldman testified that he had gone to bed the night of the murder at nine P.M., and that Mrs. Hopper had crawled into bed with him at nine-thirty that same evening. Jerome Brown, my investigator, testified that he had left Professor Goldman's apartment at nine, traveled down to the Omnibus Building and back, and would have been unable to perform the act of which Mrs. Hopper is accused within the time specified by the police. Countering this sworn statement, the District Attorney as much as accused Professor Goldman of perjury—for which Judge Kilpatrick reprimanded him. But according to the police, that is exactly what Mrs. Hopper did.

"Why did she leave the gun? Why did she use the same lipstick she had in her purse? Why was she so intent on incriminating herself and the professor? Why didn't she throw the gun into the river, so nearby, or down a sewer? Why didn't she write Sedge instead of Billy? Why, why, why? Even if, for some reason unknown to us, she intended to incriminate Professor Goldman, she was also incriminating herself.

"We hired a chemist, chief chemist at Household Research Laboratories, who testified that the note might have been written with any one of three lipsticks he produced as evidence—brands other than Devlon's Autumn. But the police were apparently not interested in alternatives. Three hundred and eighty women work in the Omnibus Building. Did the police question more than four of them before the arrest? No, they did not. Mr. William Sedgwick Hopper had a wide reputation in Boston as a womanizer. Garson, Weeds and Anderson, the firm Hopper worked for, has a Boston office. Three very attractive women travel back and forth. Did the police question them? No, they did not. The papers have been full of assertions by the firm of Garson, Weeds and Anderson that Mr. Hopper had illegally appropriated fifteen million dollars that belonged to company clients. They were waiting for their accountants to complete their audit before bringing criminal charges against Mr. Hopper. Fifteen million dollars is a lot of motive; did the police even consider that? No, they did not.

"You have listened to Elizabeth Hopper's account of the brutalities visited upon her by this cruel, sadistic monster she had married, of the hold he had over her. You heard her description of the duck blind, where she had ample opportunity to kill him. It is almost impossible to prove intent in a hunting accident. She had access to two loaded pistols in a house where many guns were kept. She could have killed him when he returned from one of his nights on the town, saying in her defense that she thought he was an intruder. Or she could have claimed self-defense during one of his drunken rages.

"Eight years of a terrible marriage proved that she is not capable of such a deed. She is a gentle, compassionate woman, a pious Catholic who never misses a Sunday at church. The police have no fingerprints, no blood samples, no DNA, no witness who saw her near the Omnibus Building—coming or going—no witness who saw her leave her apartment or reenter it. Oh, yes, they have motive, but I would guess that anyone who ever had dealings—sexual, financial, or otherwise—with William Sedgwick Hopper, has motive.

"Then what do the police have? We have proved that the lipstick as evidence is worthless. The explanation for the gun has been given by Detective Hull, and I think that we have proved to your satisfaction that revenge was not Mrs. Hopper's motive and could not be.

"I ask only that you take into account what you have seen and heard during this trial. A woman has been accused of a crime that she did not and could not commit. You are being asked the question basic to our criminal law: Can you say that Elizabeth Hopper's guilt exists beyond reasonable doubt? That's the key to all that has happened in this courtroom during this trial— reasonable doubt. If you have such reasonable doubt, you must find her innocent. That is the law. Now I thank you with all my heart for listening to me, and I know you will do what is right."

There was a small ripple of applause from the audience, which the judge quickly put an end to with his gavel and a very stern look. Sarah walked back to the table, and I leaned forward from my front-row seat and said, "Well done. Bless you." Sarah turned to look at me, suddenly old and devoid of spirit. I had never seen her quite like this before.

"I gave it my best shot."

Liz leaned over to put an arm around Sarah and kiss her. "Thank you," Liz said.

"If you're not ready, Mr. Rudge," Kilpatrick said, "we can have a short recess."

"The people are ready," Rudge replied. "Ms. Helen Slater will give the summation for the people."

That came as a small bolt out of the blue. Through the entire trial, Ms. Slater had not spoken a word, and now, suddenly, Rudge had given her the summation. From all I had heard, it was entirely unlike him. He was a dogged man who dug into each fact as if it were a piece of meat. Why then had he given the summation to Helen Slater? The only thing I could think of was that he desperately wanted to wipe out what Sarah had said and that he felt he needed a woman to face a woman. So, as they say, what goes around comes around, and here was a student of mine, ready to make a passionate plea against a woman I loved. Some of the press scurried out to make a deadline, and Kilpatrick tapped his gavel to quiet the whispering. I wondered how wise this was on the part of Rudge, and after a moment's thought decided that it was the best foot he could put forward. Men had not come off very well in Liz's testimony the day before.

I tried to recall Helen Slater the student. Certainly, I had no memory of her as she appeared now, her dark hair cut close and boyishly, a pretty face and a firm mouth. She wore a gray suit, the jacket of which hung over the back of her chair, since the air-conditioning in the court was less than perfect. Did I really remember her? Perhaps, but time had changed her. She took her place at one end of the jury box and introduced herself as Rudge's junior.

Then I remembered, but she looked so different. She had been to my home once to discuss a particular detail of contract law, and had met my son, then unmarried. He had one date with her, and when I asked him about it, he just shook his head. I recall him saying something about a woman being this hard and bitter.

Her voice was low and strong. She began by spelling out the details of the police case, and for perhaps half an hour she held forth on the people's case, and then she went into the history of the forensic laboratory of Manhattan South, of their state-of-the-art instrumentation and the detailed experience of the laboratory. A man, she claimed, would have had to wear surgical gloves to manipulate the small twenty-two pistol. A woman could do it with delicate kid gloves, and the absence of fingerprints was meaningless.

"The defense," she said, "has seen fit to throw scorn and charges of inefficiency on what is perhaps the best detective and forensic organization in the world. I don't have to defend the New York City police and I don't have to remind you of the thorough and experienced manner in which New York deals with crime. In this case, the detectives followed a narrow but obvious trail. They decided that a woman had committed the crime, not out of intuition of the single female police officer on the scene but because that is where the trail led them. Mr. Rudge put into evidence a sheet of folded computer paper that was wedged into the basement door, so that the perpetrator might return to her apartment. This is a circumstantial case, but the evidence is very clear and decisive.

"Now let me deal with Mrs. Hopper's eight years of married life. We have only her word for the scene in the duck blind. I am a woman, and I can say that if I had been subjected to the years of brutality and despair and humiliation that Mrs. Hopper received at the hands of her husband, I might well have seized a gun and put an end to it. But she did not. She waited until her emotional state had stabilized, and then she committed as cold and premeditated a crime as I have ever seen. She was no longer the woman who had sat passively in the duck blind. She was someone else. She made an appointment with her ex-husband, and he agreed to write a check made out to cash for the sum of one hundred thousand dollars. Probably, she stood behind him with the pistol at his head while he wrote the check. We offered the check in evidence. You saw the check, the quivering handwriting—everything but the signature. And then, before he could sign it or endorse it, she shot him.

"Certainly, if she had in mind only to get the money, which she well deserved, she would have taken a signed and endorsed check and left. But she had to have the cream of the jest, and she carried out his death sentence before he could sign it.

"Now, let me take up a very important psychological matter, which the defense leaned on heavily, namely the gentle, almost apologetic manner in which the defendant accepted her beating by her abusive husband, and thus forswore the several opportunities she had to kill him. You may argue among yourselves that she was incapable of murder, and possibly that was so. But was that woman the same woman you saw take the stand here? Was that a beaten, sick woman, incapable of striking back?

"This Elizabeth Hopper is another woman indeed. The months of love and care with which Professor Goldman cherished her have had their effect. Facing a possible life sentence in prison, she is firm and self-reliant. She is clear about what was done to her, and she is fully capable of taking her revenge; and that is precisely what she has done. She shot the man who abused her, a crime she worked out in advance, with precision and with expert facility. No clinging vine now. No poor, beaten woman. A thousand gypsy cabs roam the streets of New York. They cannot be traced. For a hundred dollars, they will go anywhere, anytime. What is the testimony of Investigator Brown worth? What is the testimony of when she appeared back in bed worth? At best, the time of death is never exact, but only estimated. One hundred fifteenth Street to Wall Street is between seven and eight miles. At that hour, the hour when the murder was committed, a practiced gypsy cab could be at Wall Street in fifteen minutes. Fifteen minutes there, fifteen minutes back. Time for the good professor to yawn and turn on his side.

"She played the role of a vigilante, judge, jury, and executioner, but in our society no one has the right to play those roles. Otherwise, we would live in chaos. No policeman has that right; no citizen has that right. We are a society of law, not a gunfighter's frontier town.

"You must not decide this case on the basis of sympathy for a battered wife who killed a sadistic man. You must look at the evidence and only at the evidence. This is not a case of emotional revenge or self-defense.

This is a carefully plotted and premeditated murder. There is only one question to be decided: Is Elizabeth Hopper guilty beyond a reasonable doubt?

"I know you will consider the evidence carefully, and I thank you for your patience during this trial."

It was half past one when Helen Slater finished her summation. Kilpatrick said that we would break for lunch and that court would convene in an hour, when he would charge the jury. Liz and I, and Sarah and J. J. made a gloomy foursome as we pushed through the media and down the classic steps of the Foley Square courthouse. None of us had anything to say to anyone. Jerry Brown was waiting for us, and he whisked us a few blocks uptown to Klapper's Jewish Dairy Restaurant, a place where we would be free from any reporters. There were no parking spots around, so Brown remained in the car to get us back in time. None of us was in any mood to eat, so I ordered Klapper's famous onion and potato soup for all of us, and they could taste it if they wished—although I never knew anyone to taste it and not go on with it to the end.

It was not until we had given our order that anyone spoke about the trial, and then I broke the silence by asking Sarah what she thought.

"It doesn't matter now what I think. It's up to the jury. But I must give Rudge credit for letting Slater do the closing. Knowing Rudge and his ego, I think it was an act of pure desperation. He had to have a woman speak, and I suppose he was up half the night working on it with her. What do I think of her closing? It was good, but not inspired. I don't think it changed anything."

"We have seven women on the jury," I said.

Sarah sighed. *"La donna e mobile."*

"I thought you were a feminist."

"Sometimes, Ike, sometimes. We won't get a guilty verdict—I feel sure of that, but we may get a hung jury."

"And that means a retrial?" Liz asked woefully.

"Maybe—maybe not."

"God help me, I can't go through this again." Tears filled Liz's eyes. "What am I doing to you, Ike? This has cost thousands and thousands of dollars already. Why didn't you leave me alone there on the bridge? Why didn't you let me die? I brought you nothing but misery. Sarah, if they find me guilty, what will it be? We have the death penalty now. Will it be the electric chair?"

"They will not find you guilty," Sarah said, tasting a spoonful of the soup. "Liz, for heaven's sake, taste the soup. An hour from now, Kilpatrick will be charging the jury, and he does not cherish Mr. Rudge."

"Yes," J. J. chimed in, "this is the best potato soup I ever tasted. My mama used to make soup like this, and she wasn't even Jewish."

"I should think not," Sarah said.

"How can you joke about it?" Liz pleaded.

"Because they love you, Liz," I said. "You used to tell me about your guardian angel. She'll take care of you."

"No, no, she's gone," Liz said sadly.

"Do you know what Jerry Brown found out?" J. J. said.

"How do you know what Jerry Brown found out?" asked Sarah.

"Because he took me out last week."

"Oh, J. J., you're dumber than I thought," Sarah said.

"Maybe, but Jerry found out that Kilpatrick has a married daughter who divorced her husband five years ago because he struck her."

"And you didn't tell me?" Sarah snapped.

"He said he'd mention it to you, but I guess he forgot or something."

" 'Or something.' " And when we got back into the car, Sarah said to Brown, her voice cold and steely, "Why didn't you tell me about Kilpatrick's daughter?"

"I told you," Brown protested.

"Like hell you did."

"Sure I did. I told J. J."

"This thing called the human race," Sarah said to me, "you know how it's going to end, Ike? Not by atom bombs but by sheer stupidity."

"Thank you, my love," Jerry Brown said.

Then we were back at the courthouse.

When all was in order, Kilpatrick began by pointing out that this was the most serious charge, on the people's part, that any jury could face—murder in the first degree. "You have heard the people's case and the defense's case. The people's case is based on circumstantial evidence. No one saw Elizabeth Hopper leave Professor Goldman's apartment, no one saw her in transit, no one saw her enter or leave the Omnibus Building. But there are three pieces of very strong circumstantial evidence, the gun, the lipstick, and the previous relationship of the defendant and Mr. Hopper during their marriage—which goes to motive. Now, you must not only consider the evidence, you must *weigh* the evidence. You must decide what part of the circumstantial evidence or perhaps all of it might bring you to a conclusion of guilt or innocence.

"In any capital case, the law says that to bring in a verdict of guilty, the defendant must be guilty beyond a reasonable doubt. You must consider this carefully, and if you find in your discussion and weighing of the evidence that there is a measure of reasonable doubt, you must bring in a verdict of not guilty."

It was a short but very fair charge, and certainly not a reversible charge. The jury was escorted to the jury room, and the court was adjourned.

CHAPTER ELEVEN
The Verdict

I MADE ARRANGEMENTS with Sarah that Liz and I would be at the apartment for the remainder of that first afternoon and evening of jury deliberation, and that she could call me there. After that, I had a beeper, and Sarah could find me wherever we were. Sarah assured me that there would be no verdict before the following day and probably not then, which would take us into the weekend. Jerry Brown picked us up in front of the courthouse and drove us home. Sarah and J. J. kissed Liz and said they would pray.

Liz, who had pulled herself together, said that we could have an omelet and salad for dinner, because all we needed was in the kitchen and she had no desire to leave the apartment and do grocery shopping. I agreed with her, being very tired, torn to shreds emotionally; and I said I would lie down and take a nap. I asked her whether she wanted to join me, but she said she preferred to sit at the window and look at the river, recalling the first time she had come here and how wonderful it had been.

I went into the bedroom and kicked off my shoes and sprawled out on the bed, but I couldn't sleep. I lay there thinking about how simple and normal my life had been before Liz entered it, an old widower living out his last peaceful and uninspired few years. Did I wish it had remained that way? I wondered about that. I had told Liz how lonely I was, but whether that was true or not I could not say at this point. I had a good many friends. The university where I had worked for so many years was only a short walk away; and when I lunched there, people always found me and shared my table.

My thoughts went back to that night on the bridge, when I had driven up from Rowan College in Glassboro, New Jersey. I had spent one of those rare evenings—dinner and cigars and brandy afterward— with Lewis Cohen, a physicist, and Frank Carter, a social psychologist, both of them faculty members at Rowan, a small but very respected college in South Jersey. It was one of those evenings that one treasures. My own intellectual hobby was physics, but though I read so many of the endless flow of books that appeared on the subject, I lacked the basic mathematics to understand it. Of course, their interest was contracts, and since to them I was a national authority on the subject, they kept pulling it in via the atom and its electrons as the basic contract in the universe. It was a thought I had never entertained before, although many times I had argued that contracts were basic to every system of law and order. Carter, the only one of the three of us who was not Jewish, argued that Judaism was based on a contract between man and God. A religion is always different and more esoteric to an outsider.

"I never thought of it that way," I remember saying, and then Cohen put in that Jews never think much of their religion but identify themselves to themselves on a tribal basis. I pooh-poohed that, reminding him that this so-called tribal affiliation had ceased to exist more than two thousand years ago and that Jews had long forgotten it.

"On the other hand," Carter said, "when your son was born, Ike, and when he was circumcised, he belonged to God and you had to buy him back into your family by a payment of pure gold to a priest of the temple class."

"What!" I had exclaimed. "What an absolutely barbaric notion—the last thing in the world I would descend to."

"Oh, but you did," Cohen said. "I was teaching at

Cooper Union then, and Lena asked me to come to the bris, the circumcision, because she had to have a Kohan, a priest, present. I am a Kohan, spelled Cohen in English, and if you were to go out to Long Island where three generations of my family are buried, you'd see two hands on the tombstone of each male, with the fingers spread and the thumbs touching each other. The Kohans go back to a time when the Windsors were not even a gleam in someone's eye. And that day, at your son's bris I mumbled something that had been written out for me in Hebrew, and Lena gave me her gold wedding ring, and then I returned it to her. Do you remember now?"

And to Carter, he said in the way of explanation, "Genesis, chapter one, verse twenty-two, God orders Abraham to sacrifice his son as a symbol of faith, and when Abraham agrees, God accepts the act of faith and allows the child to live. But the contract stands, that every firstborn son belongs to God and must be bought back by a Kohan with an offering of pure gold. There for Ike's profession is the first binding contract. You must remember the incident, Ike?"

And I did, but vaguely because I took no notice of it. Now, tired, emotionally bruised, and thinking of that night on the bridge, I said to myself that I had made a contract then, myself with Liz. Suddenly I was asking myself whether the contract held if Liz were guilty? Not if the verdict came in guilty, but if Liz had actually killed Hopper, regardless of what the verdict was? How I had come to this thought, I don't know. There are thoughts that reside somewhere deep in the mind; you know they are there—or at least a part of you knows that they are there—but they remain subliminal until some shock or event explodes them. Then they blow away every other thought.

I have spent most of my adult life as a teacher, but I am a lawyer—and I have lived, as I said, with a deep respect for the law. Lying on my bed in that curious haze between sleep and wakefulness, I thought again of what Frank Carter had said to me on that evening that now seemed a hundred years ago—and now I agreed with him. Contract law is the basis of all law because it is based on life itself. Everything is a contract, marriage is a contract. Criminal law is based on a contract between citizens and the state, and it is very ancient: Thou shalt not kill; thou shalt not covet thy neighbor's wife, thy neighbor's goods. The deeper memory returned, that according to the most ancient Jewish law, your child belonged to God, and when you paid the price in gold, the child was yours because you made a contract. I remembered the tears in Lena's eyes when she put the gold wedding band back on her finger.

I was a Jew by birth, not by any sort of conviction, and most of my friends who were Jewish were also Jews by birth. When my wife was alive, we lit candles on Friday night, the beginning of the Sabbath. That was the extent of our devotion. We belonged to no synagogue and we prided ourselves on being freethinkers. With Lena gone, I no longer lit candles on Friday night, and as for all the other rites and observances of Orthodox Jews, I hardly knew them—indeed, somewhat resented them as medieval superstitions. But Liz, born a Catholic, not only observed the rites, she believed in them; and if she had killed Hopper, she would have confessed it to her priest.

Liz and I had our own contract, and one of the shreds of Talmudic Judaism that remained with me was the statement that he who saves a single life saves the whole world. But what of she who takes a life?

Sarah was a brilliant litigator, but while I could not even pretend to decent litigation, I was a good lawyer. The police were not fools. They were very good at what they did, and for all that it was circumstantial, they had motive that could easily be seen as damning. Why had I refused to see that? On the other hand, what could a jury do? Sarah had only one duty—to defend her client as best she could.

I tried desperately to return such thinking into the bit of my brain where it had lain hidden all these months, telling myself that it was a conclusion that I had no right even to contemplate. I thought instead of Liz's warmth, her gentleness, and her totally innocent and, for me, wonderful caring. To think for a moment of her as a cold-blooded murderer was a deep flaw in my character.

In this mood, I dozed off, and was awakened by a soft kiss, followed by Liz's voice telling me that it was seven o'clock, and that I had been sleeping for two hours, that the eggs were ready to go into the pan, that the salad was made, and could I be ready in just three minutes?

Her tears of the afternoon were gone. Whatever she had been feeling at Klapper's, she had worked it out while I slept, and she was smiling at me. I washed my face, put on my slippers, and joined her at the table. The candles were lit, and the small supper she had prepared was delicious. I uncorked a bottle of wine, and opened a window so that we could look out at the river and watch the sun set without any reflection on the glass.

"Ike, dear Ike," she said, "dear, loyal, wonderful Ike, it's cool enough for a fire and you must light one of those prefab logs, and after dinner, we will sit in front of the fireplace and you will tell me stories about your childhood in Oneonta, where your father was Justice of the Peace. You see, I'm all right now. I have made my peace, and if they come in with a guilty verdict, I'll face it. God will know what is right and what is wrong."

"Thank God you feel that way."

"I feel that a great load has been lifted from my shoulders."

I ignited one of the prefab logs, and we sat on the couch and watched it burn and listened to Mozart— and I returned all my doubts and suspicions to that tiny spot in the back of my brain where they properly belonged. We sat with my arm around her, and when the sound of midnight came from a distant bell, we went to bed. Liz curled up next to me, warm and relaxed.

The next morning, we had coffee and toast, and then put on jeans and sweaters. With the beeper in my pocket, we walked downtown along Broadway, where on a sunny morning on a single block, half a dozen ethnic groups would be represented. Liz took no notice of the people who glanced at us curiously.

"There is no place in the whole world like the West Side here," Liz decided.

"Oh, I'm sure there is, Liz. You've never been to London."

"But someday we'll go there, won't we? If you have any money left after this trial. Poor Ike."

"I'm not poor."

"Why did I do this to you? You've spent over fifty thousand dollars on this trial, Ike. I don't know why you did it."

"Because I love you."

I suggested that we walk down Broadway to Zabar's, and Liz said that we'd be recognized. "But we're being recognized already, Liz. You see the way people look at us. This is something we're going to have to live with."

"As long as I can live with you, Ike."

She didn't mention marriage, and would not mention it until the verdict was in. The problem of being recognized lay in me, not in her. I was six feet and one inch tall, lean and craggy with a remnant of white hair. Liz, with flaxen hair, cut short and boyish now, could easily have passed without notice, but I was another matter. We altered our destination and walked over to Central Park West, where the sidewalk was almost empty at that hour, and eventually we returned to my apartment.

"Will it always be this way, Ike?"

"No. Americans remember nothing for much more than a week." I told her about a discussion in class about the Sacco and Vanzetti case—brought up, as so many cases were, even though it had no direct connection with contracts—and only the student who raised the question had ever heard of it. "And these were law students," I told her.

"I never heard of it either, Ike."

"There you are."

"But look at Jack the Ripper."

"Hardly an apt comparison. What president of the United States was accused of getting a girl pregnant while in office and, as gossip has it, was done in by his wife?"

"No, you're kidding."

"Scout's honor."

"I never heard of such a thing, and in college I had a year of American History and a year of Social Civics, as they called it then."

"The answer is Harding."

"I never heard of Harding. Who was he?"

"President of the United States, in the twenties."

"Awesome," Liz said.

"There's the great divide. Nothing was 'awesome' when I was your age."

"Because today everything is."

"Yes, I suppose so."

"What are you going to do now, Ike? This day is forever."

"I'll read the *New York Times*."

"How can you?"

"Because I know it's a sin not to."

"Then I'll sin. I wish we had a piano."

"I didn't know you played the piano, Liz. Why didn't you ever tell me?"

"Because I knew you'd run out and buy me one."

"I will, I certainly will," I assured her.

"You've spent enough money on me."

"We had a piano, but I gave it to my son after Lena died. I sent it out to the valley of the chips."

"No, no, you are not to buy me a piano. Absolutely not! What would I do with a piano in prison?"

"You're not going to prison. How many times must I tell you that?"

She threw her arms around me and wept, and the last bit of suspicion was removed from my mind. I held her and comforted her—and then the phone rang. It was Sarah, who told me that the jury had reached a decision.

"Kilpatrick will convene at two o'clock. That gives you an hour and fifteen minutes to get here. Take a cab. Is Liz with you?"

"Yes. Where are you?"

"At Foley Square. I'll stay here and pray."

"They've reached a decision," I told Liz.

She dried her eyes and I phoned the doorman for a cab. We changed clothes, and in a few minutes we were on our way downtown. Liz huddled up against me and said not a word all during the ride. She managed to smile at me when I asked her whether she was all right. Sarah and J. J. were on the broad steps of the court building, surrounded by reporters, who were prodding Sarah for her guess on the verdict.

"I don't guess," Sarah said. "We'll know soon enough."

I don't know how such word gets around, but it does; and the courtroom was packed. Jerry Brown was already there, telling Sarah, "My car's ready if the dice roll seven."

"You never told me what you're charging for all this good will," Sarah snapped.

"On the house. Maybe it'll get me a date with you."

"Maybe."

At a few minutes before two o'clock, the twelve jurors and the four alternates filed into the box. I tried to read something from their faces, but they all shared the same straightforward expression. At precisely two, Kilpatrick entered, and the clerk called out, "All rise." We all stood up, and then the judge seated himself and the audience relaxed into their seats. The forewoman of the jury, a middle-aged black woman—a registered nurse at St. Vincent's hospital—stood up.

"Madam forewoman, has the jury reached a decision?"

Both Rudge and Slater were rigid as stone. Sarah had reached out and taken Liz's hand. I had taken a seat next to Liz at the table, feeling that Kilpatrick would permit it now that the trial was over, and I took her other hand. J. J., her hands pressed together, prayed in a whisper. The court itself was silent as a tomb. "Will the defense and the people please stand," the judge said.

The forewoman held a sheet of paper. The judge nodded at the clerk, who walked to the jury box, took the sheet of paper from the forewoman, and gave it to the judge, who looked at it for a long moment and then returned it to the clerk. The clerk gave it back to the forewoman.

"In the single count of murder in the first degree, how do you find?" Kilpatrick asked.

"We find the defendant, Elizabeth Hopper, not guilty."

The judge asked Rudge whether he wanted the jury polled, but he shook his head. Then the judge thanked the jury for their service and dismissed them. He then told Liz that she was free to go.

Sarah folded Liz in her arms, and I folded both of them into my arms, and J. J. wept. I kissed Liz and I kissed Sarah, and the court broke into applause. J. J. kissed everyone. The sons and daughters of the media crowded around us, and I heard Sarah saying that it was a just verdict by a just jury, and Liz was saying that we must thank the jurors. We pushed through to the jurors and I lost sight of Liz for a moment. Sarah was saying, "Well, Professor, was I a good student?"

"The best, the very best."

Jerry Brown appeared and asked me when I wanted him to run interference for us. "I knew it," he said. "No surprise. That Sarah is something."

It was fifteen minutes or so before we got out of the building, away from the TV cameras outside, and into Brown's big Cadillac. Liz kept asking Sarah whether she was really free.

"Really free. Free as a bird."

"They can't get me back there?"

"Never. Never."

Liz curled up in my arms, and J. J. sat on the jump seat and wept again. "Because I was so frightened," she explained through her tears. "Oh, I was never so frightened in my life." She had attached herself to Liz completely. "It was like a lynching," J. J. said. "How could they even think that way about Liz?"

So it was over and Liz was free.

"When will the wedding be?" J. J. asked.

CHAPTER TWELVE

The Question

YOUTH IS IMMORTAL, which is why wars are made by old men and fought by children. But with the onset of middle age, immortality begins to crumble, and bit by bit, death begins to take shape as a reality. When you reach my age, you live with death. It becomes a close and constant companion. You may not think about it, but it is always there. Each time you lie down to sleep, a part of you is aware that you may not awaken in the morning.

When I was fourteen, walking with a friend on a dirt road on the outskirts of Oneonta, we heard a sound of a creature whimpering with pain. Poking into the brush we came upon a deer whose back had apparently been broken by an encounter with an automobile. It happened frequently enough as the deer herd increased, and we could see that the animal was in awful pain. Somehow it had dragged itself, or been hurled off the road, into the brush, and it was trying desperately to rise, moaning each time it made the effort. We knew that the only merciful thing to do was to kill it, but neither I nor my friend, whose name was Sam, had ever killed anything larger than a fish or a mosquito.

I had a hunting knife, which I carried whenever we hiked, and I thought I would take it out and cut the deer's throat. But thinking it and doing it were two different things, and after I had approached the deer—which had only two tiny velvety tips of antlers at that season—I handed the knife to Sam and told him, "You do it."

He was no more capable of slicing the poor animal's throat than I was, and finally we decided that I would stay with the deer while he found a phone and called a state trooper. It was almost an hour before the state trooper arrived, and during that time, I stood near the dying animal and listened to its whimpers of pain. It was my first real encounter with death. I had been to funerals, but the ritualistic interment of a body in a coffin was as different from this as day and night. Finally the trooper showed up, drew his pistol, and shot the deer in its head. We helped him tie the animal onto his car, and when he asked if we wanted a ride back, we shook our heads. We knew we had to walk and think about the incident, and we did think about it but said nothing to each other.

When World War II came, I enlisted as a medic before my number was called. In the Normandy landing, I went in as a stretcher carrier with another friend of mine, a boy named Kaplan, and we were told that we were going in with the first wave. Kaplan, who was fluent with Yiddish, said to me, *"Kenst gehargit verin,"* which, loosely translated means "This can kill you." It was a bitter and prophetic comment. Kaplan was a medic because, as he once told me, he could not kill—not even an insect. But he could die. He took a bullet in his belly while we were still in the surf. I had to enlist a GI to put him on the stretcher and get him to a landing ship. Kaplan died, and I was lucky enough to survive with only a bit of shrapnel in my shoulder.

All of this returned to me as I lay in bed with Liz the night of the verdict, and my resolve to put away the thoughts that had been burrowing in my brain the day before began to crumble. We had gone home to my apartment together, the five of us, Jerry Brown, Sarah, J. J., Liz, and myself; and we let the telephone ring and the answering machine pick up the messages. There was a call every five minutes or so, but I put the answering machine in a drawer and let the phone ring. It continued to ring until midnight.

Sarah sent Jerry Brown off with a list of prepared foods that he was to purchase, everything from spare-ribs to bagels and lox at Zabar's, plus four bottles of champagne at the wine shop. When he returned, Sarah spread the food on the dining-room table, and we sat around, talking and drinking and eating. Liz wanted to know how one thanked jurors, and Sarah assured her that she had already done so. Brown had picked up a late issue of the *Post,* with Sarah's picture, large, on the front page for the second time.

"Just look at that!" he chortled. "Lady, you are number one in the ofay's game. Just listen, 'Sarah Morton, tall, beautiful, and self-possessed, dominated the courthouse. As for Michael Rudge, this is good-bye to his dreams of becoming DA in the next election. He lost his nerve and turned over the summation to his associate, Helen Slater, and while she made an earnest attempt, it could not compare to Sarah Morton's passionate closing.' Now that, my lady, is damn neat, coming from a white paper."

"That wants black readers," Sarah said. "I am sick to death of the media, and blacks and whites, and racists and liberals, and all the other deep shit this society is sinking into!"

"Right on! To hell with all of it!" Brown laughed. "Let's celebrate!"

We drank to the jury, and we drank a toast to

Kilpatrick. "He gave us the verdict," I said. "How on earth the DA's office didn't pick up on his daughter and force him to disqualify himself, I don't know."

"Find a judge without a divorce in his family," Brown put in, grinning.

"What I was afraid of," Sarah said, "was that Rudge would not come in with cross-examination. That was the long chance I took. It sends shivers up my spine when I think about it. When Liz answered my single question, Rudge should have dropped it right there. But he was too eager. He opened the door, as the judge said, and we walked right in."

The talk went on, and by eleven o'clock, we decided to watch the late news on television. Liz, demolished after three glasses of champagne, declared that she couldn't keep her eyes open, so I kissed her and sent her off to bed. As we expected, the sound bites were all for the verdict, contrasting this lovely and gentle woman with the brute that had been murdered. Sarah came on the tube, being asked why she had not used the battered-wife syndrome, and she answered, "Because my client is innocent."

"Yes," I agreed when we turned off the TV, "if every battered and brutalized wife killed her husband, we would be damn near depopulated."

"What are you going to do, lady," Brown asked Sarah, "open a fancy office in midtown? There's enough business on Sugar Hill alone to pay the rent."

"I'm still a public defender on leave," Sarah replied. "Now why don't you take J. J. home, Jerry; and if you want to buy me dinner next week, I might just be available."

"Coming on top of the verdict, that's the best news I heard in a month of Sundays. Do you think you can walk, J. J.? And what about you, Sarah?"

"Ike and I have to talk. Take J. J. home. Can I have the spare room, Ike?"

"With my blessings."

I shook hands with Brown and thanked him for all he had done, assuring him that when he sent in the bill, it would be paid promptly.

"You paid me enough, Professor. No bill for the taxi service. My pleasure." At the door, he lowered his voice and said, "Do you suppose you could get me into Columbia Law School, Professor? I got three years of college credits."

"We'll talk about it."

"It might make a difference." He nodded toward Sarah.

J. J., a fixed smile on her face, hung on his arm as he left. I closed the door and went back to the dining room.

"I need coffee, Ike. And let's go into the kitchen and talk. I'm more comfortable in the kitchen."

"Keep you up if you drink coffee."

"Not with me, Ike. It keeps me alive."

I brewed a pot of strong coffee and filled my pipe. Sarah took a pack of cigarettes out of her purse. She smoked rarely, but tonight she explained that she needed it. "I have been through my own personal small hell," she admitted. "You shouldn't play three-card monte with lives."

"You won."

"Yes, I won. Life and death, and it's all a game, isn't it, Ike?"

"You called it theater."

"I never played it before with the life of someone I love."

"You love Liz?" I asked.

"She's a sweet, dear woman. And speaking of theater, Ike, what has this production cost you?"

"Close to a hundred thousand dollars."

"Yes, I guessed as much, and forty thousand of it went to me. I don't need that much, Ike. You talked me into it, but I have no joy in seeing you pauperized."

"I'm not pauperized, not by a long shot."

"Indeed? Tell me how a professor emeritus can drop a hundred grand and not feel it?"

"By buying some stock forty years ago and holding onto it. I'm not rich, Sarah, but I'm not poor either. I have a good pension, social security, and some very nice stocks and treasury bonds. I am not to be pitied. Another criminal lawyer would have been into me for at least a couple of hundred thousand and costs. I don't have many needs, Sarah. Pipe tobacco still only costs a few cents."

"Yes, but marriage may change all that. You still intend to marry Liz, don't you?"

"I think so."

"Ike, what the hell does that mean—you 'think so'?"

I remained silent for a minute or so, occupying myself with stuffing and lighting my pipe. "Sarah, I never asked you this—but I have to ask you now. Did Liz kill Hopper?"

"Why ask it at all?"

"Because I have to. That's what I am. I have to ask you."

"What makes you think I know?"

"Because you're her lawyer."

"Which," Sarah said, "makes whatever I know privileged."

I rose and closed the kitchen door, and then I said, "Jesus, Sarah, this is you and me together in the kitchen."

"I am a lawyer and you are a lawyer. Let it rest, Ike. You gave testimony that she spent the night in bed with you. How on God's earth could she have killed Hopper? Did you perjure yourself?"

"I don't know."

"You don't know whether you perjured yourself? What kind of bullshit are you giving me now—you don't know whether you perjured yourself? Where is this getting you, Ike? A jury of twelve intelligent men and women found her not guilty."

"I count my sleeping pills. I took one that night. Another was missing. I woke up that night—I don't know exactly what time it was—and she was in bed with me. Her hands were cold and she was shivering, and I put my arms around her to warm her. For God's sake, don't get angry with me, Sarah. Put yourself in my place."

"I don't want to put myself in your place. This is a rare and sweet woman. Do you have any idea of what it means to be tied to a man who brutalizes you, who demeans you constantly, who tries to destroy your soul as well as your body—and there is no escape for you?"

"Liz escaped. He could do her no more harm."

"Ike, Ike, for God's sake—did you ever strike a woman?"

"No. It's unthinkable."

"Well, it's not unthinkable for hundreds of thousands of American men, black and white. I've heard enough stories from battered wives to have no question about that. You're not a woman, and I've never met a man who has the faintest notion of what it means to be a woman in a man's world. I've never driven down Eighth Avenue and seen a line of men trying to sell their pricks for a few dollars so that they could eat or buy a snort of cocaine and make their wretched lives a little less miserable. But I've seen women doing that in every lousy city in this lousy society, and I've spoken to mothers who became whores to feed their kids or keep them in school. You goddamn men are all alike. I have spent months with Liz. She is good and pure and honest, and this is a black woman talking about a white woman. And as for William Sedgwick Hopper, he deserved to die if ever a man did, but I'm not a judge and a jury, and neither is Liz. Do you think that Liz would use your gun and leave it there? Do you think she would use her own lipstick? Do you think that Liz could be such a forsaken monster that she would incriminate you? Liz loves you so much that tears come into her eyes when she talks about you to me. Not in a thousand years could she stand behind Hopper and coldly execute him. I've met women who could, but not Liz, ever."

Sarah finished, crushed out her cigarette, and then lit another one. She breathed in the smoke, and then sat and stared at me.

"You don't think much of me, do you?"

"You don't deserve much, do you, Ike? There are over three hundred women working in the Omnibus Building. Putting Hopper in there was like letting a wolf into a flock of lambs. The cops are neither as stupid as I painted them nor as smart as TV makes them out to be. They decided they had the perp, and that was it. I blew out their lipstick theory, and the gun was stolen. Coincidence? Life is filled with coincidences. But I haven't answered your question."

"What question?"

"Did Liz kill Hopper?"

"You answered it," I said bleakly.

Sarah took a deep breath and blew out the smoke. "I hate these damn things. They're killing my voice and my voice is all I have. I'm not a paper shuffler. I'm a litigator."

"A lot more."

"No, Ike, Liz did not kill Hopper. He's still wreaking his pain inside of her, and the only one who can kill that is you, with love and kindness. Come to think about it, I'm worth every cent you paid me."

"Absolutely."

"Maybe I was too hard on you."

"Oh, no."

"Do you know why there was a sleeping pill missing? Because the first night I stayed here, I took one."

"You did," I admitted. "I had forgotten that."

"Don't eat yourself up with guilt. Your thinking was male thinking, putting yourself in place of the woman. It doesn't work. That's 'Jerry Brown sickness.'"

"What goes on between you two?"

"He wants to marry me."

"He also wants to go to Columbia Law School. He asked me for help."

"More male thinking. He wants to make himself worthy of me. Oh, shit! The hell with all of this. I'm tired, and I'm going to bed."

I got out of my clothes and crawled into bed next to Liz, kissing her very gently. I was thinking that I was an old fool and there was no fool like an old fool, but thinking no more of a deer by the roadside or World War II or the meaning of life and death and justice and injustice. Like Sarah, I was very tired, and I was twice her age.

Liz and I were married two weeks later by Judge Nussbaum, in her chambers. Present were Sarah, and my son and daughter-in-law, who had flown in from Washington the day before. They were to occupy our apartment and see New York, while we were spending a month in Europe. Liz was radiant, and there was much kissing and congratulations.

In the cab on our way to the airport, Liz said, "What was that line you quoted from the Talmud?"

"That he who saves a life saves the whole world?"

"Yes—and you see how true it is."

CHAPTER THIRTEEN
The Confession

ON JANUARY 12, 1997, Sergeant Hull was trying to work out a report on his new computer, which, courtesy of the city, had replaced his ancient Underwood typewriter. It was five o'clock in the afternoon, and Precinct One had completed an uneventful day, with nothing worse than a fight between two drunks in a tavern, a fender bender on Broadway, and an attempted suicide in a prestigious law firm. Downstairs, a woman who lived in Tribeca was wailing about the theft of her dog. Two detectives on the next shift had gone out to investigate the report of a dead homeless man on Broad Street, and Flannery had already left for home.

Lieutenant Fred Thompson opened the door of his office and beckoned Hull in.

"Can it wait? I'm trying to finish this stupid report on this stupid machine. I got to type it out and I got to print it out. What in hell they gain with these mothers I don't know."

"It can't wait," Thompson said shortly.

Hull sighed and joined Thompson.

"The Hopper case," Thompson said.

"What about the Hopper case?"

"They got a dame, name of Grace Norman, does it ring a bell?"

Hull frowned and thought about it. "Yeah, she was screwing Hopper in his home in Boston while he was still married to his wife."

"Did you or Flannery check her out?"

"The way I remember, she was in Boston. Flannery called the Boston cops."

"That's beautiful," Thompson said. "Did you check the airlines?"

Hull sighed and shook his head. "No, we didn't check the airlines. If we checked every dame Hopper screwed in Boston, we'd still be on the case. What about this Grace Norman?"

"She's in Massachusetts General Hospital in Boston, dying of AIDS. She said she murdered Hopper."

"Come on!"

"It's a dying woman's confession."

"Then we can close that lousy case. Did they fax you a copy of the confession?"

"I got the fax. I want you to go to Boston and check her out. You know the case."

"If you got the fax—"

"You can read it on the plane. It's your case, and I been on the phone with the Commissioner and the Chief of Detectives. They want the case tied up and closed. What the hell good is the confession? So she read about it in the papers. You still think the Hopper woman's the perp?"

"Yeah."

"Well, twelve good men and women think otherwise. So you get on a plane now. You see her today. Tomorrow, maybe she's dead. I got a squad car downstairs waiting to drive you to LaGuardia, and you got a police priority. I want you to see her tonight and pin her down. Take everything we got on the case with you. The Boston cops will pick you up at the airport. Leave your gun here and when you land, show your badge. I don't want any delay."

"Jesus, I don't have pajamas. I got to go home—"

"You'll be home before morning. I'll call your wife. So take off and don't give me no argument."

At seven-thirty, Hull was at Logan Airport, badge in hand. He was greeted by a policeman who introduced himself as Sergeant Gillespie.

Hull had read the confession, and had come to the

conclusion that Thompson was right. The confession read: "I, Grace Norman, do hereby state that I was responsible for the death of William Sedgwick Hopper on the night of May twenty-fourth, 1996. He gave me AIDS. I shot him."

It was neither signed nor notarized; and as a confession, Hull realized, it was utterly worthless. If that damn witch, as he often thought of Sarah, had offered it during the trial, the judge would have rejected it. As Hull brooded over it during the flight to Boston, he had become more and more convinced that he was on a fool's errand. He spent the rest of the flight time making sure that his pocket tape recorder was working properly; and the first thing he said to Gillespie was, "Is she still alive?"

Sergeant Gillespie, a stout, good-natured man, grinned and replied, "Barely."

"Breaks your heart, don't it?" Hull said.

"I ain't weeping, Inspector."

"Sergeant."

"She shot him in the back of the head after she made a deal," Gillespie said, shrugging.

"Hopper didn't have AIDS. We did a thorough autopsy. No HIV—none at all."

"You going to tell her that?"

"I don't know," Hull said. "I'll see how it goes."

"You got a tape?"

"I got one."

"I got one, too," Gillespie informed him. "I'll stick around, and after you speak to her, I'll run you back to the airport."

"It's got to be typed out, and then she has to sign it, and we got to have it notarized."

"You can write down the facts," Gillespie said. "There's a notary at the precinct. You get the main facts and the tape, it ought to be enough."

Hull followed Gillespie into the hospital, an old, tired-looking building. The policeman on duty informed them that Grace Norman was on the third floor. At the nurse's station, the woman in charge told Gillespie that Grace Norman was sleeping, that she, the nurse, was on deathwatch and they should come back in the morning.

"Suppose she's dead in the morning," Gillespie said.

"That could be, poor soul."

"This here's Inspector Hull. He just flew in from New York. He has to talk to her."

"Sergeant Hull," Hull said. "Another woman was tried for the murder she confessed to." He didn't bother to inform the nurse that Elizabeth Hopper had been acquitted.

"Oh—I see. And you have the death penalty in New York, don't you?"

"Absolutely."

"All right. We'll try." She led the two policemen down the hall and opened the door of a room where there were three beds. Two of them were empty. A woman lay in the third bed, breathing hoarsely, her eyes closed. Her head was bald except for a few hairs. Her face was ravaged, the skin sallow and clinging to the bones. It was hard for Hull to believe that this was once a woman desirable to a man like Hopper.

"Cancer and pneumonia," the nurse whispered. "They go quickly when it's both."

Grace Norman opened her eyes and stared at the three people.

"These are policemen," the nurse said. "This is Inspector Hull, my dear. He came from New York tonight to talk about your confession."

"Where is the priest?" Grace Norman managed. "I don't need cops, I need a priest." Her voice was a muted croak.

"He'll be here tonight. I promise you. After vespers."

"What do you want?" Grace Norman demanded of Hull. "Put on the light. I can't see him."

The nurse switched on the light and whispered to Hull, "She's heavily sedated, Inspector."

"We're grateful for the confession. But we must have the details. Another woman is accused of the crime."

"Who?" Grace Norman asked. "That stupid Liz? She couldn't kill a mouse. I killed that bastard. An eye for an eye, a tooth for a tooth. He gave me AIDS. He told me so, and that we shouldn't see each other again. He thought he'd walk away. But he murdered me. Now I'm dying, so get the fuck out of here and leave me alone."

Hull had pulled up a chair and was making notes on his pad. He had turned on his tape when they entered the room. As gently as he could, he said, "Please, Ms. Norman, I must have the details. When did you come to New York?"

Silence then, and finally, the nurse said, "It will do your soul good, my dear."

Silence again. Grace Norman closed her eyes. A door opened, and a priest entered the room. The nurse went to him and they whispered together. Then the nurse said to Grace Norman, "The priest is here, my dear. He will hear your confession as soon as we are finished."

"We're finished."

She motioned to the priest, who said, "No, my child, you should tell these men what they must hear."

"I confessed, Father."

"No, you will confess to me when we are alone. The weight of a murder lies on Elizabeth Hopper. You must lift that weight . . ."

Grace Norman's eyes filled with tears. Hull asked quickly, "When did you leave Boston, Ms. Norman?"

"Two days before it happened. I stayed at a hotel near the Battery, and I called him from a street phone."

"Who did you call?"

"Billy."

"You called him Billy?"

"Yes. Everyone else called him Sedge. I hated that name. He promised to buy me the biggest diamond engagement ring I had ever seen. He promised to marry me. Then he told me he had AIDS. I learned I was HIV positive, and he said that marriage made no sense anymore. Then I decided to come to New York."

"Where did you get the gun?"

"I bought it from the bellhop at the hotel. I gave him five hundred dollars for it. I told Billy I had to see him, and he told me to come to the Omnibus Building at ten o'clock that evening. He opened the door for me, and we went up to his office—" She could hardly get the words out now.

"Is it enough?" the priest asked.

"A bit more," Hull said. "What happened then?"

"We argued. He said it wasn't true that he had AIDS. He called me a whore. I took out the gun and told him to write out a check for a hundred thousand dollars, and I—I shot him before he could sign it. I couldn't have cashed it anyway, without letting the world know I killed him. Now leave me alone."

"You wore gloves?"

"Yes, kid gloves. I know about fingerprints."

"And how was the check made out?"

"Oh, God, leave me alone. Cash, cash. He never

signed it. He took it to hell with him. I looked for a sheet of paper, and then I snapped open the fax and ripped out a long sheet—" She was gasping now.

"Enough," the priest said. "For God's sake, enough."

The nurse held her up, and Hull handed her the pen, and she signed his notes. Then they left her alone with the priest.

Hull and Gillespie then went back to the station house where they had Hull's notes notarized. Gillespie signed as present witness, and then made photocopies. Hull was back in New York at Precinct One by five A.M.

SARAH TOLD MOST OF THIS to Liz and me after a visit she made to Precinct One, from her notes and from a copy of the confession that they gave her. The story had already appeared in the morning *Times,* and after I read it to Liz, she wept for a while, very quietly, curled in a corner of the couch. Then for the next hour, she was silent. I half expected her to ask me whether I had ever believed that she had killed Hopper and I wondered how I could answer that question. But she never did ask me—not then, not ever.

After that hour or so of silence, Liz said, "That poor woman. May God forgive her."

This was a woman who had slept with Liz's husband under her own roof, but I knew her well enough by now to swallow any response I might have made; instead, I mentioned that while it was cold outside, it was a beautiful day, and why didn't we take a long walk? Liz agreed, and we put on our coats and walked downtown on Riverside Drive. We never spoke about Grace Norman again.

A few days later, the District Attorney telephoned me and asked me to join him for lunch at the Harvard Club. I begged off the luncheon but agreed to stop by at his office.

"It's time for an apology," I explained to Liz.

"Don't be too hard on him, Ike. He did what he had to do."

I shrugged and made no promises. Liz was Liz. As I had said to Charlie Brown, the obligation was upon me, not upon her.

The District Attorney welcomed me into his office, and I didn't refuse his handshake. That is something you only do with people you hate. I didn't hate him. I looked upon him newly because he had long since become a stranger to me. I had known him for more than thirty years, and he was a stranger to me.

"Ike," he said, "sit down. Smoke your pipe if you wish to. We have a lot to talk about."

"Do we?"

"I think so. I'm glad this case was cleared up, better for both of us. We're old friends, Ike. Rudge is writing a letter of apology, but I felt we had to see each other and talk."

"Old friends." A thought ran through my mind, *there is no love greater than that of he who lays down his life for a friend.* "What is there to apologize for? You had the evidence, enough for a grand jury, and you had an indictment. That's the law."

"Yes, I was sure you would understand that I had no alternative."

"Ah, that begs the question, doesn't it? You took a good and pure woman—a woman so filled with grace and compassion that she turned a sour old man into a human being—and you sentenced her to death."

"Ike! Come on, you're a lawyer. You know I had no alternative."

"No alternative? You could have dropped the indictment. Your evidence was lousy. You could have demanded that the cops check the airlines. You could have checked out the hotels. You could have questioned Elizabeth about Hopper's girlfriends and sent a detective to Boston—that's only the beginning of what you could have done. But you did none of it! You had a few lousy bits of circumstantial evidence, and you pronounced a death sentence. You had an election coming up—"

He interrupted me with a growl. "Ike, you're talking nonsense, and you damn well know it!"

"No, I'm talking proof and evidence. I'm talking law. And furthermore, don't talk to me as a friend.

We're not friends. We never were." And with that, I walked out of his office, slamming the door behind me.

When Liz greeted me at the apartment, I stepped back to look at her and grinned. She was wearing a pale blue dress that we had bought together in Paris a few months ago, and to my eyes she was the loveliest woman I had ever seen.

"You're smiling," she said. "I'm glad it went well. It did, didn't it?"

"Oh yes, my dear, it went well."

"I was so afraid you'd be angry and lose your temper. But you never lose your temper. It's one of the things I love about you."

I winced visibly and stared at her.

"What is it, Ike?" she asked, alarmed by my reaction.

I shook my head. "No—absolutely not. You've never lied to me; and if this thing—you and me, Liz and Ike—is going to work, I'm never going to lie to you. It did not go well. I told him that we were not friends, when he pleaded that we were. I said he was a lousy, worthless bastard, but not in those words, and I stormed out of his office, slamming the door behind me. So that's how it went, and you might as well know the truth."

She took a long moment before she said, "Thank you, Ike—I mean for the truth. As for the rest of it—"

She shrugged and smiled. "I would have done the same thing if I had the nerve and your gift of unprintable words."

"It's totally over," I said. "Let's go somewhere for lunch and celebrate."

"I'd like that," Liz agreed.

	DATE DUE		